Arthur W. Wellington

The words of Wellington

Collected from his despatches, letters, and speeches

Arthur W. Wellington

The words of Wellington
Collected from his despatches, letters, and speeches

ISBN/EAN: 9783744715218

Printed in Europe, USA, Canada, Australia, Japan

Cover: Foto ©Raphael Reischuk / pixelio.de

More available books at **www.hansebooks.com**

THE WORDS OF WELLINGTON.

"For this is England's greatest son,
He that gain'd a hundred fights,
Nor ever lost an English gun."

ALFRED TENNYSON.

"He was the grandest, because the truest man whom modern times have produced; he was the wisest and most loyal subject that ever served and supported the English throne."—THE REV. G. R. GLEIG (*The Chaplain General*).

"The man, who, lifted high,
Conspicuous object in a Nation's eye,
Play'd in the many games of life, that one
Where what he most did value still was won.
This is the Happy Warrior; this is he
That every man in arms should wish to be."

WORDSWORTH.

THE WORDS OF WELLINGTON.

COLLECTED FROM HIS DESPATCHES,

LETTERS, AND SPEECHES,

WITH ANECDOTES,

ETC.

COMPILED BY EDITH WALFORD.

LONDON:

SAMPSON LOW, SON, AND MARSTON,

CROWN BUILDINGS, 188, FLEET STREET.

1869.

CHISWICK PRESS :—PRINTED BY WHITTINGHAM AND WILKINS,
TOOKS COURT, CHANCERY LANE.

PREFACE.

VERY little need be said of this companion volume to the "Table-Talk of Napoleon." The same Compiler has carried out the suggestion of the Editor, and has sought from a long list of works upon the great Duke, from pamphlets, reviews, and chiefly from his own despatches, letters and speeches, the opinions of him who was certainly the greatest subject who ever lived. Opposed to one who has been called by Napier "the greatest genius and the greatest soldier who ever lived," he had the happiness to conquer him; but greater than the glory of conquest was the contrast which our great General exhibited to Napoleon. One lived for himself, the other for his country; one raised himself to a throne, the other was loyally content to be a subject; one was restless in his ambition, the other always quiet in his noble subservience. The end of one was Glory, of the other Duty.

The character of the Duke of Wellington has been, curiously enough, better appreciated by M. de Brialmont than by most of his own countrymen. By the stupid mis-application of the name of a steamboat to an old and failing man, a gentle-hearted, tender, prayerful nature was mistaken for a hard and iron heart. If we choose to recollect that Wellington answered every letter that he received, even from beggars, that he gave thousands of pounds away in charity, that he never met an old soldier who had fought with him but he gave him a guinea, that he often laughed good-naturedly at the plots laid to impose upon that very *good* nature, we shall not consider him an iron Duke, and we shall learn to love as well as to venerate him.

Here in these pages the reader will find, over and over again, proofs of the great Duke's simpleness, honesty, modesty and noble-mindedness; of his truth, candour, bravery of soul; of his earnestness, foresight, hard work; of his care for his soldiers, his mental generosity to rivals, his simplicity and true greatness. He will find nothing exaggerated, indeed the records of such a life look little beside that of a more expanded and less noble hero, as a well proportioned body looks compact and small. When we consider how great were his deeds, we are struck with the modesty and the smallness of his words. His creed was in a short space: "The Lord's Prayer," he said, "contained the sum total of religion and morals," that prayer was the guide to a life whose end was "doing duty."

But short as are his sentences his utterances are weighty. They are not theatrical, not spoken for effect, but they are true ; how prophetically wise one may see by his speech on the Protestant Church, 129 *et seq.*; his warnings on the state of Ireland in the year 1834; his ideas on Trades Unions, p. 159 ; his prophecy about our Railways, p. 151 ; his simple words on the Jewish Disabilities ; and, indeed, on many other topics. So clear was his vision that his speeches of forty years ago might serve, with scarcely the alteration of a word, for "leading articles" of to-day. But not for this only are his words valuable. As he said at Waterloo, "Gentlemen, we must keep pounding away," so he keeps reiterating through life his love of truth, attachment to duty, to the straight way which must always reach its object soonest. Hence his sentences must have peculiar worth, to the young especially, in times when money is often put before honour. But the finest praise ever given to him— or to any other man—was that by the Poet Laureate in one of the noblest odes ever written, and throwing some verses of that as a wreath of eternal laurel over his name, we leave the words of this truly great man to the public :—

> His voice is silent in your council-hall
> For ever; and whatever tempests lour,
> For ever silent; even if they broke
> In thunder, silent: yet remember all
> He spoke among you, and the MAN who spoke;
> Who never sold the truth to serve the hour,
> Nor palter'd with Eternal God for power;

Who **let the** turbid streams of rumour flow
Through either babbling world of high **and low;**
Whose life was work, whose language **rife**
With **rugged** maxims hewn from life;
Who **never spoke against a foe;**
Whose **eighty winters freeze in** one rebuke
All great **self-seekers trampling on** the right:
Truth-teller was **our England's** Alfred named;
Truth-lover was **our English Duke;**
Whatever record **leap** *to* **light**
He never **shall be shamed.**

THE WORDS OF WELLINGTON.

LETTERS AND DESPATCHES.

The Marhatta Country.

 HAVE received your letter, and as I had some hand in sending you to Canara I am much concerned that your situation there is so uncomfortable to yourself. . . . This country into which I have come to visit my posts on the Marhattas frontiers is worse than that which you curse daily. It is literally not worth fighting for. . . The drubbing that we gave to the Marhattas lately has had the best effects; and although all the robbers are in motion to cut each other's throats, they treated us with the utmost hospitality, and have sent back our people, whom they had driven away. (*To Major Munro, Collector in Canara. Camp in the Province of Loo*, 8*th Oct.* 1799.)

Conduct of the Natives.

. . . I enclose the extract of a letter which I have received from Colonel Sherbrooke respecting the conduct of the amildar at Chenapatam. In my opinion the rule of proceeding between officers and amildars is, to take the most serious notice of the conduct of the former when it appears to have been such as to deserve the complaint of the latter, and never to pass over any disrespect from the amildars to the officers. Upon that principle I removed the officer from Anantpoor, of whose conduct complaint was made. . . . We well know the character of the natives of this country; when they are likely to be supported they are the most tyrannical and impudent of men, and there is no falsehood which they will not tell in support of, or as an excuse for, their conduct. (*To Lieut.-Col. Close. Seringapatam,* 15*th Dec.* 1799.)

Sir Arthur's Consideration.

I have just been down at the Laal Bang, and I find that your works are going on well. Your man had begun a wall close to the watercourse, and if that should at any time hereafter let any water through, your wall would suffer, and probably come down. I have therefore desired him to cut away half the thickness of the wall which he has begun, to leave about a foot distance between the watercourse and your wall, which may answer for a channel for the water which will ooze through, and to add to the other side of the wall the thickness which he takes from that on the side of the watercourse. If you wish it I will have this done before your return, and as walls are not very handsome, I will cover those which must be near your house with a creeper. . . . I have sent you some plantain trees, and shall have others for you when the season for cutting arrives. (*To Lieut.-Col. Close. Seringapatam,* 21*st. Dec.* 1799.)

The Amildars and the English Officers.

. . . I have just received your letter of the 24th. You are the best judge what ought to be done with the amildar at Chenapatam. Colonel Sherbrooke complains of him, and it appears by the man's own account that he had no reason to complain of the colonel. As he had a gentleman with him who understands the language, there can be no doubt of his having refused to go to Colonel Sherbrooke. This the amildar now denies; but I observe a probability that it is true, even in the excuse which he makes; namely, that he had not received orders to advance and meet him. Colonel Sherbrooke is not a man who requires all the extraordinary attentions described in your letter, nor if he did, is it probable that any of the amildars would pay them; but it is proper that he and all the officers passing the road should receive civility, and therefore it is that I wish this amildar to receive a check for his conduct, which will be an example to others. (*To Lieut.-Col. Close. Seringapatam,* 26*th Dec.* 1799.)

Consideration for Soldiers.

. . . I have long objected to sending a regiment to Chittledroog, because there is no accommodation for them, and the station has been found very unhealthy; and I am afraid that the delay of the march of the 74th will be attributed to my wish to detain them at Bangalore, instead of to its real cause. This makes me feel the disappointment more than I should otherwise. (*To Lieut.-Col. Close. Seringapatam,* 25*th Jan.* 1800.)

Fair Trading with the Natives.

. . . I approve highly of any arrangement which can be made which will give the people a fair price for their straw ; and it is to be observed that the lower it is bought, the better it is for them, provided it is sufficient to pay for the trouble of taking care of it, and to compensate them for it. As the straw is to be paid for, I agree with you that the whole of it must be forthcoming when wanted. The straw for the bullocks stands upon a different footing, and of this it is but fair that the ryots should have as much as they can use. Indeed it is taken from them for nothing only on the principle that they cannot make use of it. (*To Lieut.-Col. Close. Seringapatam, 3rd Feb.* 1800.)

Native Ideas of Time.

. . . The man first told his story ; the number of marches he made, where he halted, &c., &c. Barclay then questioned him as to the time, and made him tell at what places he had seen each new moon; and his answers have corresponded exactly with his marches and halts and his arrival here. This is a strong mark of truth, particularly in a native who knows nothing of time. (*To Lieut.-Col. Close. Seringapatam,* 15th Feb. 1800.)

The Public Service first.

I have received a letter from Lord Mornington in which he offers me the command of the troops intended against Batavia, provided Lord Clive can spare me from this country. I have written to Lord Clive upon the subject a letter which he will probably communicate to you; and I have left him to accept for me Lord Mornington's offer or not, according as he may find it most convenient for the public service, after having ascertained from the admiral the period at which he would propose to depart from the coast upon this service. The probable advantages and credit to be gained are great; but I am determined that nothing shall induce me to desire to quit this country until its tranquillity is ensured. The general want of troops however at the present moment, and the season, may induce the admiral to be desirous to postpone the expedition till late in the year. In that case it may be convenient that I should accompany him; but I beg if you have any conversation with Lord Clive you will assure him that if it should be in the smallest degree otherwise I shall be very sorry to go. (*To Josiah Webbe, Esq., Secretary to the Governor. Camp at Cuddapa, 29th May,* 1800.)

No Man a Judge in his Own Cause.

. . . No man is a competent judge in his own cause, and I shall therefore be obliged to you for your opinion upon this subject. (*To Lieut.-Col. Close. Camp at Sera, 2nd June,* 1800.)

Time.

How true it is that in military operations time is everything. (*To Lieut.-Col. Close. 30th June,* 1800.)

Public Rewards and Secret Bargains.

To offer a public reward by proclamation for a man's life, and to make a secret bargain to have it taken away are very different things: the one is to be done; the other, in my opinion, cannot, by an officer at the head of the troops. (*To Lieut.-Col. Close. Camp Right of the Werdah, 8th July,* 1800.)

"Rights of Men" Man.

. . . Our friend Munro has sent an amildar into the countries right of the Werdah who is playing the devil. He is a kind of *rights of men* man, who has ordered the people to pay no revenue to anybody, and of course is obeyed. One of the consequences of his orders is, that the peons put into the different villages and forts by the Bhow do not receive their subsistence; they have threatened to hang their havildars, and then plunder the country. (*To Lieut.-Col. Close. Camp at Soondootty, 3rd Aug.* 1800.)

Philosophical Indifference.

As for the wishes of the people, particularly in this country, I put them out of the question. They are the only philosophers about their governors that ever I met with, if indifference constitutes that character. (*To Major Munro. Camp at Hoobly, 20th Aug.* 1800.)

Breaking Strength before Attacking.

. . . Before we begin to attack a whole people we must break their strength. This can be done only by time and the expense which always attends the operations of a large army; but if the object is sufficiently great, which for many reasons it appears to be, I put the expense out of the question, and consider only the means of bringing such a body of troops upon that point as will ensure our object. (*To Lieut.-Col. Duney. Camp at Hummursagur, 4th Sept.* 1800.)

Treachery.

. . . An honest killadar of Chinnoor had written to the " King of the World" by a regular tappall, established for the purpose of giving him intelligence that

I was to be at Nowly on the 8th and at Chinnoor on the 9th. His majesty was misled by this information, and was nearer me than he expected. The honest killadar did all he could to detain me at Chinnoor, but I was not to be prevailed upon to stop; and even went so far as to threaten to hang a great man sent to show me the road, who manifested an inclination to show me a good road to a different place. My own and the Marhatta cavalry afterwards prevented any communication between his Majesty and the killadar. (*To Major Munro. Camp at Yepulpuroy, 11th Sept.* 1800.)

Fools and Knaves.

The common practice is to accuse a man of being either a fool or a knave. If he is so fortunate that it is impossible to give him the former appellation, it is certain that he will be accused of knavery. (*To Lieut.-Col. Close. Camp at Hoobly, 10th Oct.* 1800.)

Sir Arthur and Government.

. . . I have written a long letter to government this day about my departure from Ceylon, which I hope will explain everything. Whether it does or not, I shall always consider these expeditions as the most unfortunate circumstances for me, in every point of view, that could have occurred; and as such I shall always lament them. I was at the top of the tree in this country; the governments of Fort St. George and Bombay which I had served, placed unlimited confidence in me, and I had received from both, strong and repeated marks of their approbation. Before I quitted the Mysore country, I arranged the plan for taking possession of the ceded districts, which was done without striking a blow;

and another plan for conquering Wynaad and re-con-
quering Malabar, which I am informed has succeeded
without loss on our side. But this supersession has
ruined all my prospects, founded upon any service that
I may have rendered. Upon this point I must refer
you to the letters written to me and to the Governor of
Fort St. George in May last, when an expedition to
Batavia was in contemplation ; and to those written to
the governments of Fort St. George, Bombay, and Ceylon ; and to the admiral, Colonel Champagné, and myself
when the troops were assembled in Ceylon. I then ask
you, has there been any change whatever of circumstances that was not expected when I was appointed to
the command ?   If there has not (and no one can say
there has without doing injustice to the Governor-
General's foresight) my supersession must have been
occasioned, either by my own misconduct, or by an
alteration of the sentiments of the Governor-General.
I have not been guilty of robbery or murder, and
he has certainly changed his mind ; but the world,
which is always good-natured towards those whose
affairs do not exactly prosper, will not, or rather does
not, fail to suspect that both or worse have been the
occasion of my being banished, like General Kray, to
my estate in Hungary.   .   .   .   I put private considerations out of the question, as they ought and have
had no weight in causing either my original appointment or my supersession. I am not quite satisfied with
the manner in which I have been treated by government on the occasion. However I have lost neither my
health, spirits, nor temper in consequence thereof. But
it is useless to write any more upon a subject of which
I wish to retain no remembrance whatever. (*To the
Hon. H. Wellesley. Bombay*, 23rd *March*, 1801.)

PHILOSOPHY.

You will be glad to hear that I propose to leave this place for Malabar in a day or two. The Governor-General consented to my return to Mysore, if I wished it, at the same time that he said he should regret my quitting the army employed on the expedition. Upon the whole, therefore, I determined to go, notwithstanding that I was superseded in the command. When upon the point of carrying into execution this *laudable* but highly disagreeable intention, I was seized by a fever which kept me in bed for some days; and although I have now recovered, I am still weak, and am taking a remedy which prevents me from going to sea. It has therefore been impossible for me to go on the expedition, and I return to my old situation with a pleasure more than equal to the regret which I had on quitting it.[1] (*To Lieut.-Col. Close. Bombay,* 11*th April,* 1801.)

UNDESERVED DISAPPROBATION.

. . . I am concerned that the Governor-General should have any such cause of uneasiness as you describe. However it is very certain that nothing annoys a man with a feeling mind so much as the disapprobation of those whom chance has made his superiors for a short time; particularly when he knows that such disapprobation is undeserved. (*To Capt. Malcolm. Seringapatam,* 20*th Sept.* 1801.)

---

[1] To Col. Champagné on the same subject he writes: " I see clearly the evil consequences of all this to my reputation and future views; but it cannot be helped, and to things of that nature I generally contrive to make up my mind."

OPINIONS OF BRIBERY.

I have had the honour of receiving your letter of
the 15th this day, and I lose no time in replying to that
part of it in which you inform me that the Rajah or
Dessaye, of Kittoor, has expressed a wish to be taken
under the protection of the British government, and
has offered to pay a tribute to the Company, and to give
you a bribe of 4000 pagodas, and me one of 10,000
pagodas, provided this point is arranged according to
his wishes. I cannot conceive what could have induced
the Rajah of Kittoor to imagine that I was capable of
receiving that or any other sum of money as an inducement to do that which he must think improper, or he
would not have offered it. . . . I am surprised that
any man in the character of a British officer should
not have given the Rajah to understand that the offer
would be considered as an insult, and that he should not
rather have forbidden its renewal, than that he should
have encouraged it, and even have offered to receive a
quarter of the sum proposed to be given to him for
prompt payment. I can attribute your conduct upon
this occasion to nothing excepting the most inconsiderate
indiscretion, and to a wish to benefit yourself, which got
the better of your prudence. I desire, however, that
you will refrain from a renewal of the subject with
the Rajah of Kittoor at all, and that if he should renew
it you will inform him that I and all British officers consider such offers as insults on the part of those by whom
they are made. (*To* —— ——. *Seringapatam.* 20th
Jan. 1803.)

RISK.

In all great actions there is risk, which the little
minds of those who will form their judgment of your's

will readily perceive in that which I am now considering; but their remarks ought not to give you a moment's uneasiness. (*To the Governor-General. Poonah*, 21st *April*, 1803.)

THE PESHWAH.

. . God send the Peshwah soon here. My fingers itch to do something for the security of the Nizam's frontier; and till the Peshwah is established at Poonah, and his government begins to have some authority, it will not answer to alter the disposition which must insure that object, only to save a few villages from plunder. (*To Lieut.-Col. Close. Camp at Poonah*, 26th *April*, 1803.)

ORDERS FOR AN HOSPITAL.

. . . You must immediately establish an hospital, and leave in it all the sick of the Scotch brigade that require carriage. Look for some secure place for this establishment within the Nizam's frontier. If you do not do this, the first action you will have will be ruinous to you. I know that the surgeons will carry about the sick men till they die; although I am aware that generally speaking it is better to keep the sick men with their corps; but in a case of this kind, where there are so many men sick, and the carriage for the sick is so insufficient, and there is every probability that there will be more sick, an hospital must be established in which every case not on the mending hand ought to be thrown. I cannot give Mr. Kennedy any assistance of surgeons. The best man you have should be left in charge of the hospital, and the care of the corps from which you take him be given to somebody else. One gentleman will easily attend two corps. (*To Col. Stevenson. Poonah*, 2nd *May*, 1803.)

Officers' Tempers.

Captain Mackay is an honest and zealous servant of the public; but he is the most unaccommodating public officer I have ever met with. He has never failed to contrive to quarrel with the head of every other department with which he has been concerned; and I have always had the greatest difficulty in keeping matters between him and others in such a state as that the service should not be impeded by their disputes. I imagine that the difficulties between Captain Mackay and Major Symonds, to which you have alluded, are to be attributed to the state of Captain Mackay's temper; and possibly, in some degree, to a want of accommodation on the part of Major Symonds. I make no doubt but that you will have observed that this officer, also, although an excellent man, has more of the oak than the willow in his disposition. (*To Lieut.-Gen. Stuart. Poonah, 26th May,* 1803.)

Character of Indian Magnates.

. . . This ought to be a lesson to us to beware not to involve ourselves in engagements either with, or in concert with, or on behalf of, people who have no faith or no principle of honour or of honesty, or such as usually among us guide the conduct of gentlemen, unless duly and formally authorized by our government. (*To Lieut.-Gen. Stuart. Camp at Poonah,* 31*st May,* 1803.)

Character of the Peshwah.

. . . I do not believe that the Peshwah is treacherous; on the contrary, I am convinced that he sees his only safety is in the treaty with the Company; but he is incapable of transacting the business of his government; he is jealous of the influence we have acquired over his chiefs, although he knows that he owes to that influence his restoration to power; and his disposition is so vindictive that he cannot be brought to pardon those who have injured him, or to whom he has done an injury. (*To Lieut.-Gen. Stuart. Camp at Charowly, 4th June,* 1803.)

CLAIMS FOUNDED UPON SERVICE.

The gentleman you now have recommended to me is one for whom I have a respect, and in whose advancement and welfare I am materially interested, as he has been frequently recommended to me in the strongest terms by his relation, General Mackenzie, a very old friend of mine. But both you and I, my dear colonel, must attend to claims of a superior nature to those brought forward, either in consequence of our private feelings of friendship or of recommendation. Of this nature are the claims founded upon service. (*To Lieut.-Col. Close. Camp at Peepulgaum,* 3rd *July,* 1803.)

THE ENGLISH NAME DISGRACED.

What has passed in Guzerat is disgusting to a degree. The English name is disgraced, and the worst of it is that endeavours are made to conceal the disgrace under an hypocritical cant about humanity; and those feelings which are brought forward so repeatedly respecting the garrison of Parneira, are entirely forgotten in respect to the unfortunate British soldiers of the 75th and 84th Regiments who, unlike the gentlemen, submitting to be humbugged by a parcel of blackguards, are suffering in the rains. (*Camp,* 20th *July,* 1803.)

Predatory War.

A system of predatory war must have some foundation in strength, of some kind or other. (*To Lieut.-Col. Collins. Camp at Ahmednuggur, 15th Aug.* 1803.)

Real Economy.

Every attention must be paid to economy, but I consider nothing in this country so valuable as the life and health of the British soldier, and nothing so expensive as soldiers in hospital. On this ground it is worth while to incur almost any expense to preserve their lives and their health. I also request you to pay particular attention to their discipline and regularity, and to prevent their getting intoxicating liquors, which tend to their destruction. (*To Col. Murray. Camp at Seuboogaum, 21st Aug.* 1803.)

Ready for Responsibility.

I certainly am ready and willing to be responsible for any measure which I adopt, and to incur all personal risks for the public service. (*To the Governor of Bombay. Camp, 29th Aug.* 1803.)

"Acquiescence" and "Approbation."

. . . Mr. Duncan, after having acquiesced in the plan suggested by me for the organization of the troops and the plan of operations in Guzerat, has informed me that "acquiescence" did not mean "approbation," and he has detailed his objections to the general system as well as to the particulars of the plan, which go to fundamentals. I cannot understand the nice distinction between the "acquiescence" of a governor in a plan for the defence of the provinces under his government, and his "approbation" of that plan. (*To Lieut.-Col. Close. Camp at Bulgaum, 30th Aug.* 1803.)

PARTY SPIRIT.

It occurs to me that there is much party spirit in the army in your quarter; this must be put an end to; and there is only one mode of effecting this, and that is for the commanding officer to be of no side excepting that of the public; to employ indiscriminately those who can best serve the public, be they who they may, or in whatever service. The consequence will be that the service will go on; all parties will join in forwarding it and in respecting him, there will be an end to their petty disputes about trifles, and the commanding officer will be at the head of an army instead of a party. (*To Col. Murray. Camp,* 16*th Sept.* 1803.)

NATIVE MARRIAGES.

There ought to be no restriction whatever upon the princes taking as many women, either as wives or concubines, as they may think proper. They cannot employ their money in a more harmless way, and the consideration of the future expense of the support of a few more women, after their death, is trifling. Let them marry whom they please. Their marriages with Mussulmen families only create an additional number of dependants and poor connections, and additional modes of spending their money. (*Answers to Queries from Capt. Marriott at Mysore. Assye,* 26*th Sept.* 1803)

THE MOVEMENTS OF LARGE BODIES.

Large bodies move slowly, and it is not difficult to gain intelligence of their motions. A few rapid and well-combined movements made not directly upon them, but with a view to prevent the execution of any favourite design, or its mischievous consequences, soon bring them to their bearings. They stop, look about them, begin to feel restless, and are obliged to go off. In this manner I lately stopped the march of the enemy upon Hyderabad, which they certainly intended; they were obliged to return, and bring up and join their infantry; and you will have heard that in a most furious action which I had with their whole army, with one division only, on the 23rd September, I completely defeated them, taking 100 pieces of cannon, all their ammunition, &c. They fled in the greatest confusion to Burhampoor. Take my word for it, that a body of light troops will not act unless supported by a heavy body that will fight; and what is more, they cannot act, because they cannot subsist in the greater part of India at the present day. *(To Lieut.-Col. Munro. Camp, 1st Oct. 1803.)*

PRIZE MONEY.

You and I know well that there is nothing respecting which an army is so anxious as its prize money. *(To Major Shawe. Camp, 6th Nov. 1803.)*

CORRESPONDENCE.

I take the liberty to recommend as a general rule, that between those public officers by whom business can be done verbally, correspondence should be forbidden, as having a great tendency to prevent disputes upon trifling subjects, and to save the time of the public officers who are obliged, some to peruse and consider, and others to copy, those voluminous documents about nothing. *(To the Secretary of the Governor of Bombay. Camp, 11th Nov. 1803.)*

Time.

Time is everything in military operations, particularly in conducting convoys. If these come on with celerity, they run no great risk; but if they are delayed long at any place, information is given of them, and they are attacked, and the success is always a matter of doubt. (*To Major Malcolm. Camp, 15th Nov.* 1803.)

Cessation of Hostilities before Peace.

The rule not to cease from hostilities till peace is concluded is a good one in general; and I have adhered to it in practice at the siege of Ahmednuggur, and have ordered an adherence to it in all instances of that kind. But in this I think it is a rule of which the breach is more beneficial than the observance. (*To Major Shawe. Camp at Rujoora,* 23rd *Nov.* 1803.)

Submission to existing Rules.

In conducting the extensive duties with which I am charged, it has been my constant wish to conform to existing rules and establishments, and to introduce no innovations; so that at the conclusion of the war, when my duties would cease, everything might go on in its accustomed channel. (*To the Secretary of the Governor of Bombay. Camp at Ellechpoor, 5th Dec.* 1803.)

Character of the Marhattas.

It is not possible to reward these people (the Marhattas) excepting by pension. They are so depraved in their habits; their notions of justice and government are so erroneous; and they are so little to be depended

c

upon, excepting to follow their own interests, that they cannot be employed in any manner in the Company's service. (*To the Governor-General.   Camp, 15th Jan.* 1804.)

FORMATION AND DISCIPLINE OF CAVALRY.

. . . The formation and discipline of a body of cavalry arc very difficult and tedious, and require great experience and patience in the persons who attempt it. (*To Major Kirkpatrick.   Camp at Waroor, 16th Jan.* 1804.)

"PEPPER" AND WATER.

. . . P.S.—Malcolm writes from Scindiah's camp that at the first meeting Scindiah received him with great gravity, which he had intended to preserve throughout the visit. It rained violently, and an officer of the escort, Mr. Pepper, an Irishman (a nephew of old Bective's, by the bye) sat under a flat part of the tent which received a great part of the rain that fell. At length it burst through the tent upon the head of Mr. Pepper, who was concealed by the torrent that fell, and was discovered after some time by an "*Oh Jasus !*" and a hideous yell. Scindiah laughed violently, as did all the others present ; and the gravity and dignity of the durbar degenerated into a Malcolm riot ; after which they all parted upon the best terms. (*To the Marquis Wellesley.   Camp, 21st Jan.* 1804.)

DISPOSITION TO SHOW MERCY.

The war will be eternal, if nobody is to be forgiven ; and I certainly think that the British Government cannot intend to make the British troops the instruments of the Peshwah's revenge. You must decide what is to be done with this person (Baba Phurkia). I have ordered him to quit the Nizam's territories, and not to come near this army. The answer of the vakeel is natural. It is, Where is a man to go who is not allowed to remain in the territories of the Company, or of the Company's allies? When the power of the Company is so great, little dirty passions must not be suffered to guide its measures. (*To Lieut.-Col. Close. Camp at Paunchore, 22nd Jan. 1804.*)

Marhatta Truth.

The Marhattas are but little in the habit of adhering to truth; they are generally indistinct in their account of a transaction of the nature of that alluded to; and it rarely happens that those accounts are found to agree exactly with the state of the facts. (*To the Hon. M. Elphinstone with the Rajah of Berar. Camp at Yailum, 26th Jan. 1804.*)

British Moderation.

I declare that when I view the treaty of peace and its consequences, I am afraid it will be imagined that the moderation of the British Government in India has a strong resemblance to the ambition of other governments. (*To Major Malcolm. Camp, 29th Jan. 1804.*)

Long Marches.

Marches such as I have made in this war were never known or thought of before. In the last eight days of the month of October, I marched above 120 miles and passed through two ghauts with heavy guns and all the equipments of the troops, and this without injury to the efficiency of the army; and in the few days previous to this battle, when I had determined to go into Berar, I never moved less than between seventeen and twenty miles, and I marched twenty-six miles on the day on which it was fought. (*To the Hon. H. Wellesley. Camp, 40 miles N. E. from Ahmednuggur, 24th Jan.—5th Feb. 1804.*)

A Public Man's Duty.

It is necessary for a man who fills a public situation, and who has great public interests in charge, to lay aside all private considerations, whether on his own account or that of other persons. (*To Major Graham. Poonah, 2nd March, 1804.*)

Gratifying Esteem.

I have had the honour of receiving your letter of the 1st inst. in which you have announced your intention to present to me a most handsome pledge of your respect and esteem, which shall commemorate the great victory which you gained over the enemy. Be assured, gentlemen, that I never shall lose the recollection of the events of the last year, or of the officers and troops, by means of whose ability, zeal, and disciplined bravery they have in a great measure been brought about in this part of India; but it is highly gratifying to me to be certain that the conduct of the operations of the war has met with the approbation, and has gained for me the esteem of the officers under my command. (*To Lieut.-Col. Wallace, &c., and Officers of the Division of the Army in the Deccan. Camp at Poonah, 4th March, 1804.*)

Conclusion of War.

When war is concluded I am decidedly of opinion that all animosity should be forgotten, and that all prisoners should be released. (*To E. Scott Waring, Esq., Poonah. Bombay, 12th March, 1804.*)

British Good Faith.

I would sacrifice Gwalior or every frontier of India, ten times over, in order to preserve our credit for scrupulous good faith, and the advantages and honour we gained by the late war and the peace ; and we must not fritter them away in arguments drawn from overstrained principles of the laws of nations which are not understood in this country. What brought me through many difficulties in the war, and the negotiations for peace ? The British good faith, and nothing else. (*To Major Malcolm. Bombay,* 17*th March,* 1804.)

Reasonable Charity.

. . . The mode in which I propose to relieve the distresses of the inhabitants is not to give grain or money in charity. Those who suffer from famine may properly be divided into two classes; those who can and those who cannot work. In the latter class may be included old persons, children, and the sick women, who from their former situation in life have been unaccustomed to labour, and are weakened by the effects of famine. The former, viz. those of both sexes who can work, ought to be employed by the public; and in the course of this letter I shall point out the work on which I should wish that they might be employed, and in what manner paid. The latter, viz. those who cannot work, ought to be taken into an hospital and fed, and receive medical aid and medicine at the expense of the public. According to this mode of proceeding subsistence will be provided for all ; the public will receive some benefit from the expense which will be incurred ; and above all, it will be certain that no able-bodied person will apply for relief, unless he should be willing to work for his subsistence ; that none will apply who are able to work, and who are not real objects of charity ; and that none will come to Ahmednuggur for the purpose of partaking of the food which must be procured by their labour or to obtain which they must submit to the restraint of an hospital. (*To Major Graham. Bombay, 11th April,* 1804.)

SECRECY IN PUBLIC AFFAIRS.

There is nothing more certain than that of 100 affairs, 99 might be posted up at the market-cross without injury to the public interests ; but the misfortune is that where the public business is the subject of general conversation, and is not kept secret, as a matter of course, upon every occasion, it is very difficult to keep it secret upon that occasion on which it is necessary. There is an awkwardness in a secret which enables discerning men (of which description there are always plenty in an army), invariably to find it out ; and it may be depended upon, that whenever the public business ought to be kept secret, it always suffers when it is exposed to public view. For this reason secrecy is always best, and those who have been long trusted with the conduct of public affairs are in the habit of never making known public business of every description that it is not necessary that the public should know. The consequence is that secrecy becomes natural to them, and as much a habit as it is to others to talk of public matters ; and they have it in their power to keep things secret or not as they may think proper. . . . Remember that what I recommend to you is far removed .from mystery ; in fact I recommend silence upon the public business upon all occasions, in order to avoid the necessity of mystery upon any. (*To Lieut.-Col. Wallace. Camp at Niggeree,* 28*th June,* 1804.)

Unhesitating but not Unreasoning Duty.

If my services were absolutely necessary for the security of the British Empire or to ensure its peace, I should not hesitate for a moment about staying, even for years; but these men or the public have no right to ask me to stay in India, merely because my presence, in a particular quarter, may be attended with convenience. (*To Major Shawe. Seringapatam, 4th Jan. 1805.*)

Difficulty in tracing Causes.

. . . It must ever be difficult to trace exactly the causes of the influence of one power over the councils of another; particularly for a person who has not a very accurate knowledge of characters. (*To Lieut.-Col. Kirkpatrick. Seringapatam, 19th Jan. 1805.*)

Modesty.

I have no confidence in my own judgment in any case in which my own wishes are involved. I mistrust the judgment of every man in a case in which his own wishes are concerned. (*To Major Shawe. Seringapatam, 3rd Feb. 1805.*)

The Existing Government.

I don't think that this Government can last very long: you can have no idea of the disgust created by the harshness of their measures, by the avidity with which they have sought for office, and by the indecency with which they have dismissed every man supposed to have been connected with Pitt. (*To Lieut.-Col. Malcolm. London, 25th Feb. 1806.*)

Both Sides of the Question.

It frequently happens that the people who do commit outrages and disturbances have some reason to complain ; but in my opinion that is not a subject for the consideration of the general officer. (*To Brig.-Gen. Lee. Cork, 7th July,* 1808.)

Sentiments in favour of the Spanish.

It is impossible to convey to you an idea of the sentiment which prevails here in favour of the Spanish cause. The difference between any two men, is whether the one is a better or a worse Spaniard, and the better Spaniard is the one who detests the French most heartily. I understand that there is actually no French party in the country, and at all events I am convinced that no man now dares to show that he is a friend to the French. (*To Visct. Castlereagh. Corunna, 21st July,* 1808.)

Foolishness of Pushing Raw Troops forward.

There is nothing so foolish as to push half disciplined troops forward ; for the certain consequence must be, either their early and precipitate retreat if the enemy should advance, or their certain destruction. (*To Lieut.-Col. Frant. Lavos, 6th Aug.* 1808.)

Vimiero.

The action of Vimiero is the only one I have ever been in, in which everything passed as was directed, and no mistake was made by any of the officers charged with its conduct. (*To H.R.H. the Duke of York. Vimiero, 22nd Aug.* 1808.)

Astonishment at Abuse.

You will readily believe that I was much surprised when I arrived in England to hear of the torrents of abuse with which I had been assailed ; and that I had been accused of every crime of which a man can be guilty except cowardice. I have not read one word that has been written on either side, and I have refused to publish, and don't mean to authorize the publication of a single line in my defence. (*To the Duke of Richmond. London,* 10*th Oct.* 1808.)

Dissatisfaction in an Army.

We are not naturally a military people, the whole business of an army upon service is foreign to our habits, and is a constraint upon them, particularly in a poor country like this. This constraint naturally excites a temper ready to receive any impressions which will create dissatisfaction ; and when dissatisfaction exists in an army, the task of the commander is difficult indeed. I am therefore most desirous that the reasonable grounds for it, which do now exist, should be removed ; and I have pointed out one of two modes in which this object can be effected. (*To the Right Hon. J. Villiers. Coimbra,* 30*th May,* 1809.)

The British Army.

I have long been of opinion that a British army could bear neither success nor failure. *To the Right Hon. J. Villiers. Coimbra, May* 31*st,* 1809.)

Provost Duty.

. . . There ought to be in the British army a regular provost establishment, of which a proportion should be attached to every army sent abroad. All the foreign armies have such an establishment, the French *Gendarmerie Nationale*, to the amount of thirty or forty with each of their corps; the Spaniards their *policea militar*, to a still larger amount; while we, who require such an aid more, I am sorry to say, than any of the other nations of Europe, have nothing of the kind excepting a few sergeants, who are taken from the line for the occasion, and who are probably not very fit for the duties which they are to perform.

The authority and duties of the provost ought, in some manner to be recognized by the law. By the custom of British armies, the provost has been in the habit of punishing on the spot (even with death, under the orders of the commander-in-chief), soldiers found in the act of disobedience of orders, of plunder, or of outrage. There is no authority for this practice, excepting custom, which I conceive would hardly warrant it; and yet I declare that I do not know in what manner the army is to be commanded at all, unless the practice is not only continued, but an additional number of provosts appointed.

There is another branch of this subject which deserves serious consideration. We all know that the discipline and regularity of all armies depend upon the diligence of the regimental officers, particularly the subalterns. I may order what I please, but if they do not execute what I order, or if they execute it with negligence, I cannot expect that British soldiers will be orderly or regular. There are two incitements to men of this description to do their duty as they ought; the fear of punishment and the hope of reward. As for the first, it cannot be given individually; for I believe I should find it very difficult to convict any officer of doing this description of duty with negligence, more particularly as he is to be tried by others, probably guilty of the same offence. But these evils of which I complain are committed by whole corps; and the only way in which they can be punished is by disgracing them, by sending them into garrison, and reporting them to His Majesty. I may and shall do this by one or two battalions, but I cannot venture to do it by more ; and then there is an end to the fear of this punishment, even if those who received it were considered in England as disgraced persons rather than martyrs.

As for the other incitement to officers to do their duty zealously, there is no such thing. We who command the armies of the country, and who are expected to make exertions greater than those made by the French armies, to march to fight, and to keep our troops in health and in discipline, have not the power of rewarding or promising a reward for a single officer of the army ; and we deceive ourselves, and those who are placed under us, if we imagine we have that power, or if we hold out to them that they shall derive any advantage from the exertion of it in their favour. (*To Visct. Castlereagh. Abrantes*, 17th *June*, 1809.)

Spanish Difficulties.

It is not a difficult matter for a gentleman in the situation of Don M. de Garay, to sit down in his cabinet and write his ideas of the glory which would result from driving the French through the Pyrenees ; and I believe there is no man in Spain who has risked so much, or who has sacrificed so much to effect that object, as I have. But I wish that Don M. de Garay, or the gentlemen of the Junta, before they blame me for not doing

more, or impute to me beforehand the probable consequences of the blunders or the indiscretion of others,
would either come or send here somebody to satisfy the
wants of our half-starved army, which, although they
have been engaged for two days, and have defeated twice
their numbers, in the service of Spain, have not bread
to eat. It is positively a fact, that during the last seven
days, the British army have not received one-third of
their provisions ; that at this moment there are nearly
4,000 wounded soldiers dying in the hospital in this
town from want of common assistance and necessaries,
which any other country in the world would have given
even to its enemies ; and that I can get no assistance of
any description from the country. I cannot prevail
upon them even to bury the dead carcasses in the neighbourhood, the stench of which will destroy themselves
as well as us. (*To the Right Hon. J. H. Frere. Talavera de la Reyna, 31st July,* 1809.)

ENTHUSIASM.

People are very apt to believe that enthusiasm carried the French through their revolution, and was the
parent of those exertions which have nearly conquered
the world ; but if the subject is nicely examined, it will
be found, that enthusiasm was the name only, but that
force was the instrument which brought forward those
great resources under the system of terror, which first
stopped the allies ; and that a perseverance in the same
system of applying every individual and every description of property to the service of the army by force, has
since conquered Europe. (*To Visct. Castlereagh. Me-
rida, 25th Aug.* 1809.)

Soldiers' Worship.

. . . The soldiers of the army have permission to go to mass so far as this; they are forbidden to go into the churches during the performance of Divine service, unless they go to assist in the performance of the service. I could not do more, for in point of fact, soldiers cannot by law attend the celebration of mass, excepting in Ireland. The thing now stands exactly as it ought; any man may go to mass who chooses, and nobody makes any inquiry about it. The consequence is that nobody goes to mass, and although we have whole regiments of Irishmen, and of course Roman Catholics, I have not seen one soldier perform any one act of religious worship in these Catholic countries, excepting making the sign of the cross to induce the people of the country to give them wine. Although, as you will observe, I have no objection, and they may go to mass if they choose it, I have great objections to the inquiries and interference of the priests of the country to induce them to go to mass. The orders were calculated to prevent all intrigue and interference of that description; and I was very certain that when the Irish soldiers were left to themselves either to go or not, they would do as their comrades did, and not one of them would be seen in a church. I think it best that you should avoid having any further discussion with the priests on this subject; but if you should have any, it would be best that you should tell them what our law is, and what the order of this army. Prudence may then induce them to refrain from taking any steps to induce the Roman Catholic soldiers to attend mass; but if it should not, and their conduct should be guided by religious zeal, I acknowledge, that however indifferent I should have been at seeing the soldiers flock to the churches under my orders, I should not be very well satisfied to see them filled by the influence of the priests, taking advantage of the mildness and toleration which is the spirit of that order. (*To the Right Hon. J. Villiers. Badajoz, 8th Sept.* 1809.)

ACCOMMODATION.

. . . Half the business of the world, particularly that of our country, is done by accommodation and by the parties understanding each other ; but when rights are claimed they must be resisted if there are no grounds for them ; when appeal must be made to higher powers there can be no accommodation ; and much valuable time is lost in reference, which ought to be spent in action. (*To the Right. Hon. J. Villiers.* (*Badajoz, 20th Sept.* 1809.)

POPULAR ASSEMBLIES.

I acknowledge that I have a great dislike to a new popular assembly. Even our own ancient one would be quite unmanageable, and in these days would ruin us, if the present generation had not before its eyes the example of the French Revolution; and if there were not certain rules and orders for its guidance and government, the knowledge and use of which render safe, and successfully direct its proceedings. (*To Marquis Wellesley. Badajoz, 22nd Sept.* 1809.)

AN HONOURABLE ACQUITTAL.

It is difficult and needless at present to define in what cases an honourable acquittal by a Court Martial is peculiarly applicable; but it must appear to all persons to be objectionable, in a case in which any part of the transaction which has been the subject of investigation before the Court Martial, is disgraceful to the character of the party under trial. A sentence of honourable acquittal by a Court Martial should be considered by the officers and soldiers of the army as a subject of exultation; but no man can exult in the termination of any transaction, a part of which has been disgraceful to him. And although such a transaction may be terminated by an *honourable* acquittal by a Court Martial, it cannot be mentioned to the party without offence, or without exciting feelings of disgust in others: these are not the feelings which ought to be excited by the recollection and mention of a sentence of honourable acquittal. (*To Brig.-Gen. Slade. Lisbon,* 12th *Oct.* 1809.)

MILITARY ETIQUETTE.

I who have arrived pretty nearly at the top of the tree should be the last man to give up any points of military right or etiquette. . . . The battle of Talavera was certainly the hardest fought of modern days, and the most glorious in its result to our troops. Each side engaged lost a quarter of its numbers. It is lamentable that owing to the miserable inefficiency of the Spaniards, to their want of exertion, and the deficiency of numbers even of the allies, much more of discipline and every other military quality when compared with the enemy in the Peninsula, the glory of the action is the only benefit which we have derived from it. But that is a solid and substantial benefit of which we have derived some good consequences already; for strange to say I have contrived with the little British army to keep everything in check since the month of August last; and if the Spaniards had not contrived by their own folly, and against my entreaties and remonstrances, to lose an army in La Mancha, about a fortnight ago, I think we might have brought them through the contest. As it is, however, I do not despair. I have in hand a most difficult task, from which I may not extricate myself; but I must not shrink from it. I command *an unanimous army*; I draw well with all the authorities in Spain and Portugal; and I believe I have the good wishes of the whole world. In such circumstances one may fail, but it would be dishonourable to shrink from the task. (*To Col. Malcolm. Badajoz*, 3rd Dec. 1809.)

The Common Council and Wellington.

. . . I see that the Common Council of the city of London have desired that my conduct shall be inquired into; and I think it probable that the answer which the King will give to this address will be consistent with the approbation which he has expressed of the acts which the gentlemen wish to make the subject of inquiry; and that they will not be well pleased. I cannot expect mercy at their hands, whether I succeed or fail; and if I should fail, they will not inquire whether the failure is owing to my own incapacity, to the blameless errors to which we are all liable, to the faults or mistakes of others, to the deficiency of our means, to the serious difficulties of our situation, or to the great power and abilities of our enemy. In any of these cases I shall become their victim; but I am not to be alarmed by this additional risk, and whatever may be the consequences, I shall continue to do my best in this country. (*To the Earl of Liverpool. Pombal*, 2nd June, 1810.)

Dedication Scruples.

. . . I have no objection to any gentleman dedicating to me his work, but I cannot give my formal sanction to his doing so, without reading and considering the work, and seeing whether it is of a nature to deserve that recommendation to the public. I have not leisure for this, and I therefore return the gentleman's paper. (*To the Right Hon. J. Villiers. Coimbra, 6th Jan.* 1810.)

What the Honour and Interest of the Country require.

. . . I conceive that the honour and interests of the country require that we should hold our ground here as long as possible; and please God, I will maintain it as long as I can; and I will neither endeavour to shift from my own shoulders on those of the ministers the responsibility of the failure by calling for means which I know they cannot give, and which, perhaps, would not add materially to the facility for attaining our object; nor will I give to the ministers, who are not strong, and who must feel the delicacy of their own situation, an excuse for withdrawing the army from a position which, in my opinion, the honour and interest of the country require they should maintain as long as possible. I think that if the Portuguese do their duty, I shall have enough to maintain it; if they do not, nothing that Great Britain can afford can save the country; and if from that cause I fail in saving it, and am obliged to go, I shall be able to carry away the British army. (*To the Right Hon. J. Villiers. Viseu, 14th Jan.* 1810.)

Going "like a Gentleman."

When we do go, I feel a little anxiety to go like gentlemen out of the hall door, particularly after the pre-

D

parations I have made to enable us to do so, and not out of the back door, or by the area. (*To the Earl of Liverpool. Viseu, 2nd April,* 1810.)

THE AUSTRIAN MARRIAGE.

The Austrian marriage is a terrible event, and must prevent any great movement on the Continent for the present. Still I do not despair of seeing at some time or other a check to the Buonaparte system. Recent transactions in Holland show that it is all hollow within, and that it is so inconsistent with the wishes, the interests, and the existence of civilized society, that he cannot trust even his brothers to carry it into execution. If the Spaniards had acted with common prudence, we should be in a very different situation in the Peninsula, but I fear there are now no hopes. (*To Brig.-Gen. R. Craufurd. Viseu, 4th April,* 1810.)

DESERTION.

Till lately desertion from a British army on service was a crime almost unknown, and I am concerned to add that I have reason to believe that many of those who have deserted have been guilty of the worst description of that offence, and have gone over to the enemy. I attribute the prevalence of this crime in a great measure to the bad description of men of which many of the regiments are composed almost entirely, and who have been received principally from the Irish militia. . . . I attribute the desertion from this army likewise in some degree to the irregular and predatory habits which those soldiers had acquired who having straggled from their regiments during the late service under the command of Sir J. Moore, were some of them taken prisoners by the

French, and have since escaped from them; and others, after having wandered in different parts of Portugal and Spain, have returned to the army. All these men have shifted for themselves in the country by rapine and plunder, since they quitted their regiments in 1808; and they have informed others of their modes of proceeding, and have instilled a desire in others to follow their example, and live in the same mode and by the same means, free from the restraints of discipline and regularity. (*To the Adjutant-General of the Forces. Viseu, 6th April*, 1810.)

WAR.

. . . War is a terrible evil, particularly to those who reside in those parts of the country which are the seat of the operations of hostile armies; but I believe it will be found upon inquiry, and will be acknowledged by the people of Portugal, that it is inflicted in a less degree by the British troops than by the others; and that eventually all they get from the country is paid for, and that they require only what is necessary. (*To Brig.-Gen. Cox. Celorico*, 14*th May*, 1810.)

OFFICIAL DISCUSSIONS.

. . . I conceive that a part of my business, and perhaps not the most easy part, is to prevent discussions and disputes between the officers who may happen to serve under my command. (*To Brig.-Gen. R. Craufurd. Celorico*, 29*th May*, 1810.)

CLAIMS FOR PROMOTION.

. . I have never been able to understand the principle on which the claims of gentlemen of family, fortune, and influence in the country, to promotion in the army, founded on their military conduct and character and services should be rejected, while the claims of others, not better founded on military pretensions, were invariably attended to. It would be desirable certainly that the only claim to promotion should be military merit ; but this is a degree of perfection to which the disposal of military patronage has never been, and cannot be, I believe, brought in any military establishment. The commander-in-chief must have friends, officers on the staff attached to him, &c., who will press him to promote their friends and relations, all doubtless very meritorious, and no man can at all times resist these applications ; but if there is to be any influence in the disposal of military patronage, in aid of military merit, can there be any in our army so legitimate as that of family connexion, fortune and influence in the country. . . . In all services excepting that of Great Britain, and in former times in the service of Great Britain, the Commander-in-Chief of an army, employed against the enemy in the field, had the power of promoting officers, at least to vacancies occasioned by the service, in the troops under his own command ; and in Foreign services the principle is carried so far, as that no person can venture to recommend an officer for promotion belonging to an army employed against the enemy in the field, excepting the Commander of that army. . . . It is not known to the army and to strangers, and I am almost ashamed of acknowledging, the small degree (I ought to say nullity) of power of reward which belongs to my situation ; and it is really extraordinary that I have got on so well without it ; but the day must come when this system must be altered. (*To Lieut.-Col. Torrens, Military Secretary. Celorico,* 4*th Aug.* 1810.)

Necessity for Secrecy.

Officers have a right to form their own opinions upon events and transactions; but officers of high rank or situation ought to keep their opinions to themselves ; if they do not approve of the system of operations of their commander, they ought to withdraw from the army. (*To Charles Stuart, Esq. Gouvea, 11th Sept.* 1810.)

Colin Campbell.

In respect to Colin Campbell, I shall add that you have been misinformed or I am much mistaken. Before I came to Portugal the first time, the Duke of York promised both Lord Wellesley and me that he would promote him to be a Major, in answer to our recommendations solely on account of his services. . . . I never intended to say that I was not obliged by the Commander-in-Chief's attention to the claims of Colin Campbell to promotion ; but I asserted, and with due submission to superior authority must maintain, that he had claims which, independent of any recommendation of mine, must have promoted him. (*To Lieut.-Col. Torrens, Military Secretary. Gouvea, 15th Sept.* 1810.)

Punishment.

Many of the assertions of these persons may have been perfectly true, although imprudent at the moment ; and I must say that I think it is not just in the Government to punish and stigmatize people for words spoken which are only imprudent. . . . That which is required in the Government is to punish those guilty of neglect and malversation in office, those who disobey or delay to obey orders, and those who neglect or delay, or omit to perform the duty of their situations. (*To Dom. M. Forjaz. Busaco, 24th Sept.* 1810.)

TRANQUILLITY.

All I ask from the Portuguese Government is tranquillity in the town of Lisbon, and provisions for *their own troops;* and as God Almighty does not give 'the race to the swift, or the battle to the strong,' and I have fought battles enough to know, that even under the best arrangements, the result of any one is not certain, I only beg that they will adopt preparatory arrangements to take out of the enemy's way those persons who would suffer if they were to fall into his hands. (*To Charles Stuart, Esq. Rio Maior,* 6*th Oct.* 1810.)

NATIONAL DISEASE OF SPAIN.

The national disease of Spain, that is, boasting of the strength and power of the Spanish nation till they are seriously convinced that they are in no danger, then sitting down quietly and indulging their national indolence. (*To the Right Hon. H. Wellesley. Cartaxo,* 2*nd Dec.* 1810.)

INFLUENCE OF NEWSPAPER PARAGRAPHS.

I hope that the opinions of the people in Great Britain are not influenced by paragraphs in newspapers, and that those paragraphs do not convey the public opinion or sentiment upon any subject. Therefore I (who have more reason than any public man of the present day to complain of libels of this description) never take the smallest notice of them; and have never authorized any contradiction to be given, or any statement to be made in answer to the innumerable falsehoods, and the heaps of false reasoning, which have been published respecting me and the operations which I have directed. I admit,

however, that others may entertain a different opinion
of the effect of these libels, and that they may not have
nerves or temper to hear or to see their conduct misrepresented and their actions vilified ; and if you should
not be convinced that these paragraphs have made no
impression, and are not the representation of the public
opinion in England, I have no objection to your making
any use you think proper of this and my former letters ;
and you may be assured that I shall be happy to avail
myself of every opportunity of bearing testimony to the
zeal, ability, and success, with which the duties of the
medical department of this army have been invariably
carried on under your superintendence. (*To Dr.
Franck. Cartaxo, 7th Jan.* 1811.)

The Portuguese.

There is something very extraordinary in the nature
of the people of the Peninsula. I really believe them,
those of Portugal particularly, to be the most loyal and
best disposed, and the most cordial haters of the French
that ever existed; but there is an indolence and a want
even of the power of exertion in their disposition and
habits, either for theirown security, that of their country,
or of their allies, which baffle all our calculations and
efforts. (*To Charles Stuart, Esq. Cartaxo,* 16*th Jan.*
1811.)

Anonymous Letters.

. . . *Baron* Eben has made some curious disco-
veries at Lisbon, and has given Mr. Stuart some papers
written by those personages (Principal Sousa and the
Bishop), which tend to show their folly equally with
their mischievous dispositions. Among other plans they
have one for libelling and caricaturing me in England.

They complain that you and I have had hunting parties! and that I eat a good dinner at Oporto instead of pursuing Soult: I have this day discovered that some of the anonymous letters to me are written by the Principal, and I suspect others by the Bishop. But this last is not quite so clear. These are men to govern a nation in difficult circumstances. (*To Marshal Sir W. C. Beresford, K.B. Cartaxo, 3rd March,* 1811.—11 *a.m.*)

Libellous Nonsense.

I return Stockler's paper, which I have not had leisure to read. The Government may publish any nonsense they please. It is entirely a matter of indifference to me; but I think they had better take care how they endeavour to set the people of the country against those who have saved them. They are much mistaken if they think they can do me any harm by such nonsense, or that they can themselves stand for a moment after they shall have convinced the people that the English, and I in particular, have not done my best for them. You know best whether these opinions can be brought forth. I am entirely indifferent whether they can or not, or what becomes of Stockler and his book. (*To Charles Stuart, Esq. Lonzao,* 16*th March,* 1811.)

Correspondence of Officers.

. . . I am sure your Lordship does not expect that I or any other officer in command of a British army, can pretend to prevent the correspondence of the officers with their friends. It could not be done if attempted, and the attempt would be considered an endeavour by an individual to deprive the British public of intelligence of which the Government and Parliament do not choose to deprive them. I have done everything in my power by way of remonstrance, and have been very handsomely abused for it ; but I cannot think of preventing officers from writing to their friends. This intelligence must certainly have gone from some officer of this army, by whom it was confidentially communicated to his friends in England ; and I have heard that it was circulated from one of the officers with a plan. (*To the Earl of Liverpool. Lonzao*, 16*th March*, 1811.)

Spanish Conduct of Marches.

The conduct of the Spaniards throughout this expedition is precisely the same as I have ever observed it to be. They march the troops night and day without provisions or rest, and abusing everybody who proposes a moment's delay to afford either to the famished and fatigued soldiers. They reach the enemy in such a state as to be unable to make any exertion, or to execute any plan, even if any plan had been formed ; and then, when the moment of action arrives, they are totally incapable of movement, and they stand by to see their allies destroyed, and afterwards abuse them because they do not continue unsupported exertions to which human nature is not equal. (*To Lieut.-General Graham. Sta. Marinha*, 25*th March*, 1811.)

Cool Judgment.

The desire to be forward in engaging the enemy is not uncommon in the British army ; but that quality which I wish to see the officers possess, who are at the head of the troops, is a cool, discriminating judgment in action which will enable them to decide with promptitude how far they can and ought to go with propriety ;

and to convey their orders and act with such vigour and decision, that the soldiers will look up to them with confidence in the moment of action, and obey them with alacrity. *To Major-General Alex. Campbell. Villa Formosa, 15th May, 1811.)*

INCREASED DIFFICULTY OF POSITION.

. . . I certainly feel every day more and more the difficulty of the situation in which I am placed. I am obliged to be everywhere, and if absent from any operation something goes wrong. It is to be hoped that the general and other officers of the army, will at last acquire that experience which will teach them that success can be attained only by attention to the most minute details; and by tracing every part of every operation from its origin to its conclusion, point by point, and ascertaining that the whole is understood by those who are to execute it. (*To the Earl of Liverpool. Villa Formosa, 15th May,* 1811.)

DYING OF LOVE.

. . . We read occasionally of desperate cases of this description, but I cannot say that I have ever yet known of a young lady dying of love. They contrive in some manner to live and look tolerably well, notwithstanding their despair and the continued absence of their lover; and some even have been known to recover so far as to be inclined to take another lover, if the absence of the first has lasted too long. I don't suppose that your protegée can ever recover so far, but I do hope that she will survive the continued necessary absence of the major, and enjoy with him hereafter many happy days.[1] (*To —— ——. Quinta de S. Joao, 27th June,* 1811.)

Anonymous Letter-writing.

To send an anonymous letter to anybody is to accuse him of writing it, the meanest action certainly of which any man can be guilty. (*To his Excellency C. Stuart. Quinta de S. Joao, 1st July,* 1811.)

The Delivery of Orders.

. . . What the troops want should be issued to them as soon as it reaches the regiments, and the means of conveyance should be delivered to the commissariat to be applied to other purposes. Obedience to this order may sometimes be attended by inconveniences, but they are trifling in comparison with the inconveniences which all would suffer from a disobedience of it. (*To Major-Gen. R. Craufurd. Portalegre,* 30*th July,* 1811.)

The Military Character of the Portuguese.

. . . The people of Portugal in general are agriculturists, and like those of the same description in all other countries, are very little disposed to military service. As I have before stated they are obliged by the ancient law of their country to serve, otherwise, I believe, that very few of them would be found in the ranks, and they are very much addicted to desertion (not to the enemy) in their own country, as well as in Spain. In Lisbon and Oporto some recruits might be got; but to show your lordship how few, I may mention that an

---

[1] The major afterwards married the young lady who was dying of love for him. He returned to the army, and was mortally wounded at the battle of Vittoria.

attempt was made, under the patronage of the present patriarch, to raise the Lusitanian legion by enlistment, instead of by conscription, and two battalions were never completed; and their losses by desertion were so great, and their gains by recruiting by the mode of enlistment so small, that in a very few months after they were raised it was necessary to give up the mode of recruiting by enlistment, and to allot the Lusitanian legion to one of the provinces, to be completed with recruits raised within the same by conscription. (*To the Earl of Liverpool. Pedrogao, 4th Aug.* 1811.)

On the Subject of Favours received.

I have just received your letter of the 20th July, in which you apprise me of the impression so unfavourable to me in a certain quarter, from my having omitted to make my acknowledgments of the support I had received, and particularly for having been allowed to recommend a certain number of officers for promotion. . . You were quite correct in stating that I had expressed my acknowledgments to the office whence the communication had proceeded; and if reference is made to the office of the commander-in-chief, it will be found that on the 14th May I did express what I felt upon the particular subject of the promotion of the officers, not in cold terms. It may be wrong to consider public arrangements not as matters of favour to any individual, and therefore not fit subjects for the acknowledgments of that individual, and at all events I don't see in what manner, or in what terms, an individual like me is to address the head of the nation upon such an occasion. Even if I had received a mark of personal favour I should doubt the propriety of my addressing my acknowledgments direct to so high

an authority, and if it be true that the support of the war in the Peninsula is a public arrangement, I should be apt to consider an address of acknowledgment from me as misplaced, if not something near impertinence.
. .   I hope that His Royal Highness will believe that he has not in his service a more zealous or a more faithful servant than myself.   I shall serve him to the best of my ability as long as he may think I can promote his service ; and his Royal Highness will find that I shall not ask for his favour at all for myself, and I hope not unreasonably for those under my command who have a right to expect that I should make known their pretensions. (*To* —— ——. *Penamacor, 6th Aug.* 1811.)

Want of Spirit.

The instances of want of spirit among the officers are very rare, and the example of punishment for this crime is not required.   This being the case, I should wish to avoid giving the soldiers and the world a notion that an officer, and particularly one belonging to a foreign nation, can behave otherwise than well in the presence of the enemy; and if there should be an unfortunate person who fails in this respect, I would prefer to allow him to retire to a private station, rather than expose his weakness. (*To H.S.H. the Duke of Brunswick.   Fuente Guinaldo, 29th Aug.* 1811.)

Officers require to be kept in order.

. . .   I must also observe that British officers require to be kept in order, as well as the soldiers under their command, particularly in a foreign service.   The experience which I have had of their conduct in the Portuguese service has shown me that there must be an authority, and that a strong one, to keep them within due bounds; otherwise, they would only disgust the soldiers over whom they should be placed, the officers whom they should be destined to assist, and the country in whose service they should be employed. (*To the Earl of Liverpool, Richoso, 1st Oct.* 1811.)

Military Clothing.

I hear that measures are in contemplation to alter the clothing, caps, &c., of the army. There is no subject of which I understand so little; and abstractedly speaking I think it indifferent how a soldier is clothed, provided it is in a uniform manner, and that he is forced to keep himself clean and smart, as a soldier ought to be. But there is one thing I deprecate, and that is any imitation of the French in any manner.

It is impossible to form an idea of the inconveniences and injury which result from having anything like them either on horseback or on foot, and our piquets were taken in June because the 3rd Hussars had the same caps as the French *chasseurs à cheval* and some of their Hussars; and I was near being taken on the 25th September from the same cause.

At a distance, or in action, colours are nothing; the profile and shape of a man's cap and his general appearance are what guide us; and why should we make our people look like the French? A *cocked tailed* horse is a good mark for a dragoon, if you can get a good side view of him; but there is no such mark as the English helmet, and as far as I can judge, it is the best cover a dragoon can have for his head. I mention this because in all probability you may have something to say to these alterations; and I only beg that we may be as different

as possible from the French in everything. The narrow
top caps of our infantry, as opposed to their broad top
caps, are a great advantage to those who are to look at
long lines of posts opposed to each other. (*To Lieut.-
Col. Torrens, Military Secretary. Freueda, 6th Nov.*
1811.)

BUONAPARTE'S TYRANNY.

I have long considered it probable that even *we* should
witness a general resistance throughout Europe to the
fraudulent and disgusting tyranny of Buonaparte created
by the example of what has passed in Spain and Portugal; and that *we* should be actors and advisers in
these scenes; and I have reflected frequently upon the
measures which should be pursued to give a chance of
success.

Those who embark in projects of this description
should be made to understand, or to act as if they understood, that having once drawn the sword they must not
return it till they shall have completely accomplished
their object. They must be prepared and must be
forced to make all sacrifices to the cause. Submission
to military discipline and order is a matter of course;
but when a nation determines to resist the authority, and
to shake off the Government of Buonaparte, they must
be prepared and forced to sacrifice the luxuries and
comforts of life, and to risk all in a contest which, it
should be clearly understood before it is undertaken,
has for its object to save all or nothing.

The first measure for a country to adopt is to form
an army and to raise a revenue from the people to defray
the expense of the army. Above all, to form a Government of such strength as that army and people can be
forced by it to perform their duty. This is the rock

upon which Spain has split, and all our measures in any other country which should afford hopes of resistance to Buonaparte should be directed to avoid it. The enthusiasm of the people is very fine and looks well in print, but I have never known it produce anything but confusion. In France, what was called enthusiasm, was power and tyranny, acting through the medium of popular societies, which have ended by overturning Europe, and establishing the most powerful and dreadful tyranny that ever existed. In Spain, the enthusiasm of the people spent itself in *vivas* and vain-boasting. The notion of its existence prevented even the attempt to discipline the armies; and its existence has been alleged ever since as the excuse for the rank ignorance of the officers, and the indiscipline and constant misbehaviour of the troops.

I therefore earnestly recommend you, wherever you go, to trust nothing to the enthusiasm of the people. Give them a strong and a just and, if possible, a good Government; but above all, a strong one, which shall enforce them to do their duty by themselves and their country; and let measures of finance to support an army go hand in hand with measures to raise it. (*To Lieut.-Gen. Lord W. Bentinck. Freueda*, 24*th Dec.* 1811.)

ALBUERA.

The battle of Albuera was fought on the 16th May, on the ground pointed out. That which was most conspicuous in the battle of Albuera, was the want of discipline of the Spaniards. These troops behaved with the utmost gallantry, but it was hopeless to think of moving them. In the morning the enemy gained an eminence which commanded the whole extent of the line of the allies, which either was occupied or was intended to be occupied by the Spanish troops. The natural operation would have been to re-occupy this ground by means of the Spanish troops, but that was impossible. The British troops were consequently moved there; and all the loss sustained by those troops was incurred in regaining a height, which ought never for a moment to have been in possession of the enemy. After the battle of Albuera, the enemy retired leisurely to Llerena and Guadalcaual. (*From the Memorandum of Operations in* 1811. *Freueda,* 31*st Dec.* 1811.)

CIVIL EDITING OF MILITARY MATTERS.

The license to publish anything upon military operations, whether true or not, which results from the liberty of the press, is a very great inconvenience, particularly to an army comparatively small, which must seize opportunities to avail itself of favourable circumstances, &c., &c. But that inconvenience is increased tenfold when a military official body publish a newspaper containing statements and observations upon military transactions. Any editor may happen to stumble upon a fact or reasoning, of which it would be important for the enemy to have information; but the staff, the official editors, must be supposed to have the information which they publish. (*To the Right Hon. H. Wellesley. Freueda,* 9*th Feb.* 1812.)

SHRAPNEL'S SHELLS.

I enclose the answer which I have received from Marshal Sir W. Beresford on the reference made to him by your Lordship's desire, respecting the value of the spherical case-shot called, "Shrapnel's Shells." Since I wrote to your Lordship on that subject, I have heard that they

E

have been very destructive to the enemy in Badajoz, when thrown from 24-pounder carronades; and I have directed that some of them may be loaded with musket-balls, in order to remedy what I have reason to believe is a material defect in these shells, viz.—that the wounds which they inflict don't disable the person who receives them, even for the action in which they are received. (*To the Earl of Liverpool. Camp before Badajoz, 3rd April,* 1812.)

Gallantry of Troops.

It is impossible that any expressions of mine can convey to your Lordship the sense which I entertain of the gallantry of the officers and troops upon this occasion. The list of killed and wounded will show, that the general officers, the staff attached to them, the commanding and other officers of the regiments put themselves at the head of the attacks which they severally directed, and set the example of gallantry which was so well followed by their men. (*To the Earl of Liverpool. Camp before Badajoz, 7th April,* 1812.)

Foreign Notions of British Invincibility.

The Spanish nation and troops, particularly the common soldiers, entertain an opinion that our soldiers are invincible; and that it is only necessary that they should appear in order to insure success; and they are so ignorant of the nature of a military operation that they attribute our refraining from interfering upon many occasions, to disinclination to the cause, and frequently to the want of the requisite military qualities in the general officer who directs our operations. (*To Major-Gen. Cooke. Fuente Guinaldo,* 1812.)

Foundation of Discipline.

The foundation of every system of discipline which has for its object the prevention of crimes, must be the non-commissioned officers of the army. (*To the Earl of Liverpool. Fuente Guinaldo*, 10*th June*, 1812.)

Galloping Cavalry.

I have never been more annoyed than by —— ——'s affair, and I entirely concur with you in the necessity of inquiring into it. It is occasioned entirely by the trick our officers of cavalry have acquired of galloping at everything, and their galloping back as fast as they gallop on the enemy. They never consider their situation ; never think of manœuvring before an enemy ; so little that one would think they cannot manœuvre excepting on Wimbledon Common, and when they use their arm as it ought to be used, viz. offensively, they never keep nor provide for a reserve.

All cavalry should charge in two lines, one of which should be in reserve ; if obliged to charge in one line, at least one-third should be ordered beforehand to pull up and form in second line, as soon as the charge should be given, and the enemy has been broken and has retired. (*To Lieut.-Gen. Sir R. Hill, K.B. Salamanca*, 18*th June*, 1812.)

Public Credit.

When a nation is desirous of establishing public credit, or in other words, of inducing individuals to confide their property to its government, they must begin by acquiring a revenue equal to their fixed expenditure ; and they must manifest an inclination to be honest, by performing their engagements in respect to their debts. (*To His Excellency C. Stuart. Salamanca,* 25th *June,* 1812.)

THE COMMISSARIAT.

The commissariat is a public department under the particular charge and direction of the commissary general and his officers ; and no officer of the army, be his rank what it may, has a right as a matter of course to interfere in its duties. I don't mean to say that the general officers and their staff are not to superintend the performance of their duties by the officers of all the departments of the army attached to the particular division of troops placed under their command ; but the duty of a general and his staff in respect to these departments is confined to superintendence ; he cannot give directions because he is not responsible for the performance of the duty of the department, and when his interference goes beyond superintendence, he is liable to be thrown upon his own justification. (*To —— ——. Rueda,* 7th *July,* 1812.)

SALAMANCA.

I hope that you will be pleased with our battle (Salamanca).   There was no mistake ; everything went on as it ought ; and there never was an army so beaten in so short a time. If we had had another hour or two of daylight not a man would have passed the Tormes ; and as it was they would all have been taken if Don Carlos de España had left the garrison in Alba de Tormes as I wished and desired ; or having taken it away, as I believe before he was aware of my wishes, he had informed me that it was not there. If he had I should have marched in the night upon Alba where I should have caught them

all, instead of upon the fords of the Tormes. But this
is a little misfortune which does not diminish the honour
acquired by the troops in the action, nor I hope the advantage to be derived from it by the country ; as I don't
believe there are many soldiers who were in that action
who are likely to face us again till they shall be very
largely re-inforced indeed. (*To Earl Bathurst. Flores
de Avila, 24th July*, 1812.)

THE SPANISH AND FRANCE.

It is impossible to describe the joy manifested by the
inhabitants of Madrid upon our arrival, and I hope that
the prevalence of the same sentiments of detestation of
the French yoke, and of a strong desire to secure the
independence of their country, which first induced them
to set the example of resistance to the usurper, will induce them again to make exertions in the cause of their
country, which, being more wisely directed, will be more
efficacious than those formerly made. (*To Earl Bathurst.
Madrid, 13th Aug.* 1812.)

SPANISH ENERGY.

I don't expect much from the exertions of the Spaniards notwithstanding all that we have done for them.
They cry *viva* and are very fond of us and hate the
French; but they are in general the most incapable of
useful exertion of all the nations that I have known ;
the most vain, and at the same time the most ignorant,
particularly of military affairs, and above all of military
affairs in their own country. I can do nothing till General Castanos shall arrive, and I don't know where he is.
I am afraid that the utmost we can hope for is, to teach

them how to avoid being beat. If we can effect that object, I hope we might do the rest. (*To Earl Bathurst. Madrid, 18th June,* 1812.)

Opinions on Withdrawal from Spain.

If for any cause I should be overpowered or should be obliged to retire, what will the world say? What will the people of England say? What will those in Spain say? That we had made a great effort attended by some glorious circumstances; and that from January 1812, we had gained more advantages for the cause, and had acquired more extent of territory by our operations, than had ever been gained by any army in the same period of time, against so powerful an enemy; but that being unaided by the Spanish officers and troops, not from disinclination, but from inability on account of the gross ignorance of the former, and the want of discipline of the latter, and from the inefficiency of all the persons selected by the Government for great employment, we were at last overpowered, and compelled to withdraw within our own frontier. (*To the Right Hon. Sir H. Wellesley, K.B. Madrid,* 23rd *Aug.* 1812.

Proclamation.

Spaniards! it is unnecessary to take up your time by recalling to your recollection the events of the last two months, or by drawing your attention to the situation in which your enemies now find themselves. Listen to the accounts of the numerous prisoners daily brought in, and deserters from their army; bear the details of the miseries endured by those who, trusting to the promises of the French, have followed the vagabond fortunes of the usurper, driven from the capital of your monarchy; hear these details from their servants and followers, who have had the sense to quit this scene of desolation, and if the sufferings of your oppressors can soften the feeling of those inflicted upon yourselves, you will find ample cause for consolation.

But much remains still to be done to consolidate and secure the advantages acquired. It should be clearly understood that the pretended king is a usurper, whose authority it is the duty of every Spaniard to resist; that every Frenchman is an enemy, against whom it is the duty of every Spaniard to raise his arm.

Spaniards! you are reminded that your enemies cannot much longer resist; that they must quit your country if you will only omit to supply their demands for provisions and money, when those demands are not enforced by superior force. Let every individual consider it his duty to do everything in his power, to give no assistance to the enemy of his country, and that perfidious enemy must soon entirely abandon in disgrace a country which he entered only for the sake of plunder and in which he has been enabled to remain only because the inhabitants have submitted to his mandates, and supplied his wants.

Spaniards! Resist this odious tyranny, and be independent and happy. (*Madrid, 29th Aug.* 1812.)

HONOURS.

I shall receive with gratitude any honour which His Royal Highness may think proper to confer upon me, but the addition proposed to my arms is the last which would have occurred to me. It carries with it an appearance of ostentation, of which I hope I am not guilty; and it will scarcely be credited that I did not apply for it. (*To Earl Bathurst. Valladolid, 18th Sept.* 1812.)

SOLDIERS' COMPLAINTS.

It is a great error to suppose that the lower orders are always right in their complaints, and the higher orders always in the wrong. My experience has taught me that nine times in ten, the soldiers loudest in their complaints and claims, have no ground for either the one or the other, and are generally in debt to their captains. There is no point in the service to which I have at all times paid so much attention as to the settlement of the soldiers' accounts; I consider early settlements to be essential to discipline. (*To Col. Torrens, Military Secretary. Torquemada*, 13*th Sept.* 1812.)

AN ESTATE IN ENGLAND.

When the Prince Regent promoted me in the peerage last Spring, and made an addition to my pension, I determined for the sake of my sons to lay out all the money I had in the purchase of land in Great Britain, and I directed that inquiries might be made for a suitable purchase for me. I likewise intend to lay out in the same manner the sum of money which His Royal Highness has declared his intention to recommend to Parliament to grant me. The inquiries which have been made, have not hitherto produced any favourable result, and I could not make any purchase with which I should be so well satisfied as that on which you have written to me. I am ready, therefore, to pay the money as soon as I shall receive your answer to this letter. I am rather inclined, however, to wish to receive the estate and manor as a gift from the public as part of the £100,000 if your Lordship should see no objection; but if there should be any, I shall be too happy to make the purchase out of my private funds.

While writing upon this subject it occurs to me that as I propose to lay out all the money which the public will grant me in the purchase of land in Great Britain, it would save me some trouble, and might probably be more advantageous to the public, if the value were granted in land. However, I suggest this to your lordship to be attended to only in case there should be no objections. (*To the Earl of Liverpool, First Lord of the Treasury. Revilla, 15th Sept. 1812.*)

The Effect of the Revolution in Spain.

It is extraordinary that the revolution in Spain should not have produced one man with any knowledge of the real situation of the country. It really appears as if they were all drunk, and thinking and talking of any other subject but Spain. How it is to end God knows! (*To the Right Hon. Sir H. Wellesley, K.B. Rueda, 1st Nov. 1812.*)

A Kind Letter.

I was very sorry that you fell the victim of great and persevering indiscretion, and misapplication of very good talents; and I am happy to find that you are sensible of your error, and desirous of beginning your career again, with a determination to avoid the conduct in future which has occasioned your misfortunes. (*To ———, Esq., late Lieut. ——— Dragoons. Cuidad Rodrigo, 21st Nov. 1812.*)

Review of the Campaign.

From what I see in the newspapers I am much afraid that the public will be disappointed at the result of the last campaign, notwithstanding that it is in fact the most successful campaign in all its circumstances, and has produced for the cause more important results than any campaign in which a British army has been engaged for the last century. We have taken by siege Cuidad Rodrigo, Badajoz, and Salamanca; and the Retiro surrendered. In the meantime the allies have taken Astorga, Guadalacara, and Consuegra, besides other places taken by Duran and Sir H. Popham. In the months elapsed since January this army has sent to England little short of 20,000 prisoners, and they have taken and destroyed, or have themselves the use of the enemy's arsenals in Cuidad Rodrigo, Badajoz, Salamanca, Valladolid, Madrid, Astorga, Seville, the lines before Cadiz, &c.; and upon the whole we have taken and destroyed, or we now possess little short of 3,000 pieces of cannon. The siege of Cadiz has been raised, and all the countries south of the Tagus have been cleared of the enemy. . . . The fault of which I was guilty in the expedition to Burgos was, not that I undertook the operation with inadequate means, but that I took there the most inexperienced, instead of the best troops. I left at Madrid the 3rd, 4th, and light divisions, who had been with myself always before, and I brought with me all that were good, the 1st division, and they were inexperienced. In fact, the troops ought to have carried the exterior line by escalade on the first trial on the 22nd September, and if they had we had means sufficient to take the place. They did not take the line because ——, the field officer who commanded, did that which is too common in our army. He paid no attention to his orders, notwithstanding the pains I took in writing them, and in reading and explaining them to him twice over. He made none of the dispositions ordered; and instead of regulating the attack as he ought, he rushed on as if he had been the leader of a forlorn hope, and fell

together with many of those who went with him. He
had my instructions in his pocket; and if the French
got possession of his body, and were made acquainted
with the plan, the attack could never be repeated.
When he fell, nobody having received orders what to
do, nobody could give any to the troops. I was in the
trenches, however, and ordered them to withdraw.
Our time and ammunition were then expended, and our
guns destroyed in taking this line, than which at former
sieges we had taken many stronger by assault.

I see that a disposition already exists to blame the
Government for the failure of the siege of Burgos. The
Government had nothing to say to the siege. It was
entirely my own act. In regard to means, there were
ample means, both at Madrid and at Santander, for the
siege of the strongest fortress. That which was wanting
at both places was means of transporting ordnance and
military stores to the place where it was desirable to
use them. The people of England, so happy as they are
in every respect, so rich in resources of every description, having the use of such excellent roads, &c., will not
readily believe that important results here frequently
depend upon fifty or sixty mules, more or less, or a few
bundles of straw to feed them; but the fact is so. (*To
the Earl of Liverpool. Cuidad Rodrigo, 23rd Nov. 1812.*)

DISCIPLINE.

The discipline of every army, after a long and active
campaign, becomes in some degree relaxed, and requires
the utmost attention on the part of the general and
other officers to bring it back to the state in which it
ought to be for service; but I am concerned to have to
observe that the army under my command has fallen off
in this respect in the late campaign to a greater extent

than any army with which I have ever served, or of which I have ever read. Yet this army has met with no disaster; it has suffered no privations which but trifling attention on the part of the officers could not have prevented, and for which there existed no reason whatever in the nature of the service; nor has it suffered any hardships excepting those resulting from the necessity of being exposed to the inclemencies of the weather at a moment when they were most severe. . . . We must therefore look for the existing evils and for the situation in which we now find the army, to some cause besides those resulting from the operations in which we have been engaged.

I have not hesitation in attributing these evils to the habitual inattention of the officers of the regiments to their duty, as prescribed by the standing regulations of the service, and by the orders of the army.

I am far from questioning the zeal, still less the gallantry and spirit of the officers of the army, and I am quite certain that if their minds can be convinced of the necessity of minute and constant attention to understand, recollect, and carry into execution the orders which have been issued for the performance of their duty, and that the strict performance of this duty is necessary to enable the army to serve the country as it ought to be served, they will in future give their attention to these points.

Unfortunately the inexperience of the officers of the army has induced many to consider that the period during which an army is on service is one of relaxation from all rule instead of being, as it is, the period during which of all others every rule for the regulation and control of the conduct of the soldier, for the inspection and care of his arms, ammunition, accoutrements, necessaries and field equipments, and his horse and horse appointments; for the receipt and issue and care of his provisions, and the regulation of all that belongs to his food and the forage for his horse, must be most strictly attended to by the officers of his company or troop, if it is intended that an army, a British army in particular, shall be brought into the field of battle in a state of efficiency to meet the enemy on the day of trial. (*To Officers Commanding Divisions and Brigades. Freueda, 28th Nov.* 1812.)

Inconveniences arising from change of Officers.

I have frequently mentioned to you the great inconvenience which I felt from the constant change of officers in charge of every important department, or filling every situation of rank or responsibility with this army. No man can be aware of the extent of this inconvenience who has not got this great machine to keep in order and to direct, and together with the British army, the Spanish and Portuguese concerns, the labour which these constant changes occasion is also of the most distressing description. No sooner is an arrangement made, the order given, and the whole in a train of execution, than a gentleman comes out who has probably but little knowledge of the practical part of his duty in any country, and none whatever in this most difficult of all scenes of military operation. Nobody in the British army ever reads a regulation or an order as if it were to be a guide for his conduct, or in any other manner than as an amusing novel, and the consequence is, that when complicated arrangements are to be carried into execution (and in this country the poverty of its resources renders them all complicated), every gentleman proceeds according to his fancy; and then, when it is found that the arrangement fails (as it must fail if the order is not strictly obeyed) they come upon me to set matters to rights, and thus my labour is increased tenfold. (*To Col. Torrens, Military Secretary.   Freueda, 6th Dec.* 1812.)

INDEPENDENT AUTHORITIES.

Experience has shown, that, wherever there exist authorities independent of each other, they must clash and the service must suffer, unless their acts should be vigilantly controlled by the superintending authority of the Government. I shall not contend for the expediency of the contrary practice in a well-regulated state, but it cannot be expected that any province of Spain should be in a state fit to be governed according to the best principle, viz. the separation of the local authorities. Even in countries where these systems and principles are perfectly understood, and have been put in practice for centuries, and of which the tranquillity has not lately been disturbed by a foreign enemy, it has frequently been necessary to place the military and political authority in one hand. How much more necessary, therefore, must it be in provinces just recovered from the usurpation of the enemy, in which the authority of the Government is imperfectly established, with which the Government has but little if any communication, to provide against the clashing of independent authorities in the administration of the local affairs? (*To the Minister at War.   Cadiz, 27th Dec.* 1812.)

SECOND IN COMMAND.

I am glad that your ideas and mine agree about your military situation. It is certain that Government have always thought it necessary to have an officer here, selected by them to succeed to the command, in case I should be deprived of it; and there are some of the Government so partial to old practice and precedent, that they don't like a departure from either, in not calling this officer *second in command.* This officer might have been very useful in the days of councils of war, &c.; it may look well in a newspaper to see that such a general officer is "second in command." But there is nobody in a modern army who must not see that there is no duty for the second in command to perform, and that this office is useless. It is at the same time inconvenient, as it gives the holder pretensions which can't be gratified except at the public inconvenience. (*To Marshal Sir W. C. Beresford, K.B. Freueda*, 10th *Dec.* 1812.)

OLD SOLDIERS AND RAW RECRUITS.

Experience has shown us in the Peninsula, that a soldier who has got through one campaign is of more service than two, or even three, newly arrived from England; and this applies to the cavalry equally with every other description of troops. (*To H. R. H. the Commander-in-Chief. Cadiz*, 26th *Dec.* 1812.)

REMOVAL OF INCAPABLE OFFICERS.

I don't exactly comprehend that part of your letter which relates to the removal of —— ——, —— ——, —— ——, ——, and —— ——, from this country. I don't understand what responsibility attaches to the removal of officers from situations which they are supposed incapable of filling, particularly from situations of comparatively subordinate rank. Odium may attach to the person who removes them without otherwise providing for them; but I don't believe that either his Royal Highness or I could ever be called upon as public men to account for the removal of any of them.

I feel strongly, and others under my command feel still more strongly, the inconvenience of being obliged to employ some at least of the officers above mentioned, but in every letter which I have ever written upon a subject of this description, I have protested against anything harsh being done to the officer who I wished should be removed.   I have not by me at present the copy of my letter to you upon the subject of these officers, and I can't be certain that it did not contain the same request, and I keep his Royal Highness's orders by me till I shall see whether it does or not.   If it does not, I beg to refer the order for his further consideration, and to request that none of these officers should be removed unless his Royal Highness has it in his power to employ them on the home staff or elsewhere.

I don't mean to alter my report of them in any degree when I state that I believe them all to be zealous in the service; but in my opinion and in the opinion of those under me, and who are more immediately in communication with them, they are not fit for their situations; at the same time I wish they should not be removed unless they can be otherwise provided for.   I beg that it may be understood that I am ready to bear all the responsibility or odium which can attach to the person who causes their removal. (*To Col. Torrens, Military Secretary.   Niza,* 22nd *Jan.* 1813.)

MAJESTY.

I wish that some of our reformers would go to Cadiz, to see the benefit of a sovereign's popular assembly calling itself Majesty; and of a written constitution; and of an executive Government called " Highness," acting under the control of " His Majesty," the assembly! In truth there is no authority in the state, excepting the libellous newspapers; and they certainly ride over both Cortes and Regency without mercy. (*To Earl Bathurst. Freueda,* 27*th Jan.* 1813.)

A Fortunate Man.

I have written to His Royal Highness to thank him for my appointment to be Colonel of the Blues. I believe there never was so fortunate or so favoured a man. (*To Colonel Torrens, Military Secretary. Freueda,* 31*st Jan.* 1813.)

Slovenly Business Ways.

As far as I have any knowledge of the sentiments of the King's ministers I believe them to be well disposed towards you, and the omission to which you advert, unaccountable as it is, must be attributed to that kind of negligent, slovenly mode of doing business which is too common among public men in England. (*To Marshal Sir W. C. Beresford, K.B. Freueda,* 16*th Feb.* 1813.)

Honourably Acquitted.

. . . I likewise return the proceedings on the trials of Hospital mates ——, ——, and ——, for the same reason, and in order that the Court may revise their sentence.

These three gentlemen were charged with a drunken riot at Coimbra, of the existence of which there is undoubted evidence on the face of the proceedings; and yet because none of the facts charged are proved against one of the three, the Court have thought proper *honourably* to acquit him. I should wish the Court to consider whether it is possible that there can be any honour in the conduct of any man in a riot by a drunken party of

F

which he is one.   His conduct may have been an exception to that of others, but it is quite impossible that it should be honourable. (*To Major-Gen. Baron Brock. Freueda, March* 20, 1813.)

French Government.

From what I know of the French system of government I entertain no doubt of its being very oppressive, and that all thinking men in any country in which it is established must be desirous of getting rid of it. But the question amongst these must always be in what manner, and at the expense of what exertions; and there are many, probably the majority of this class, who would prefer to trust to the chapter of accidents, to involving themselves and their country in the dangers and losses of a general insurrection; and by far the greater majority of the people in those countries, particularly those in easy circumstances, would prefer to pass their lives quietly under any system of government, however oppressive, to making any sacrifices, or any exertions, in order to get rid of it. I believe this to be the case in Italy; and I have not seen any proof of the existence of a general desire to get rid of the French government; nor have I ever been able to learn the names of any principal men, or ever to discover that in any particular town there existed men of talents and influence who had anything to say to this supposed insurrection.

The question of insurrection in any country must always be one of great doubt; but it appears to me that if such a measure should be adopted by any country, at any time, it ought to be adopted by Germany at present. It appears that the people cannot be in a worse situation than they are; their enemy is humbled, and there is a formidable and victorious army on the frontier ready to give support to their efforts. But those who are about to involve their country in these troubles, must not imagine that their task is an easy one, or that the contest or its evils will be of short duration. They little know the character of their enemy, and have studied his conduct but little, if they don't expect a most vigorous contest if once they draw the sword, and are not prepared as he is to endure everything, and to go to all extremities to attain their object. (*To Earl Bathurst. Freueda,* 21*st March,* 1813.)

An Inadmissible Doctrine.

. . . I can't but observe, upon —— ——'s complaint that he is to be placed at the disposal of a foreign tribunal, that the notion is too common among the officers and soldiers of the army, that they are not obliged to obey the laws of the country in which they are acting; or, in other words, that they may act as they please, and may commit such outrages as they think proper, provided they don't offend against the Mutiny Act, and Articles of War. I can't, however, admit of such a doctrine; and —— —— will be an instance that the laws of the country must be obeyed if the Portuguese government shall desire that he may be delivered over to the tribunals of that country. (*To Lieut.-Gen. the Hon. Sir G. L. Cole, K.B. Freueda,* 25*th March,* 1813.)

The Influence of Woman.

—— is a weak foolish creature, who did not know what he was about, or the mischief he was doing. I am astonished that —— should be so anxious about him, but I conclude that this anxiety has some relation to the sick lady; and one can only lament that he should be another instance of the influence possessed by women over the most sensible men. (*To the Right Hon. Sir H. Wellesley, K.B. Freueda, 4th May, 1813.*)

Duty without Mortification.

. . . I acknowledge that I cannot understand the nature of the feelings of an officer which are to be mortified by his performance of his duty in the situation in which His Majesty and the rules of the service have placed him ; and I can only say that in the course of my military life, I have gone from the command of a brigade to that of my regiment, and from the command of an army to that of a brigade or division, as I was ordered, without feeling any mortification. (*To Col. —— ——. Freueda, 10th May, 1813.*)

British Orders.

Having received from Sir Thomas Graham the Insignia of the Order of the Garter, I enclose a letter from Lady Wellington, containing directions for returning to the Genealogist of the Bath the Collar and Badge of that order. Some of my brother officers, however, have expressed an anxious desire that I should continue a Knight of the Bath, into which I have admitted most of them, and all of them owe this honour to actions performed under my command. Under these circumstances, and adverting to the reasons which induced you to wish that I should resign the order, I would wish you to consider whether it would not be better that I should keep it : first, there is a precedent of a British subject holding two British orders, neither of them military, in the case of the Duke of Roxburgh ; secondly, if you will refer to the Statute of the Order of May 1812, you will see that upon my resignation you have not the power of appointing a Knight of the Bath. My stall will be filled by the Senior Extra Knight, and under the Statute you may appoint as many extra knights as you please.

I feel great reluctance in suggesting that I should keep this order, and should not have done so if it had not been suggested to me by some of the knights. God knows I have plenty of orders; and I consider myself to have been most handsomely treated by the Prince Regent and his Government, and shall not consider myself the less so, if you should not think proper that I should retain the Order of the Bath. I beg you will return me the enclosed letter or not, as you may decide upon this point.

Believe me, &c., WELLINGTON.

(*To the Earl of Liverpool. Freueda*, 12th *May*, 1813.)

THE PRINCE OF ORANGE.

The Prince of Orange appears to me to have a very good understanding, he has had a very good education, his manners are very engaging, and he is liked by every person who approaches him : such a man may become anything; but, on the other hand, he is very young, and can have no experience in business, particularly in the business of revolutions; he is very shy and diffident; and I don't know that it will not be a disadvantage to him to place him in a situation in which he is to be at the head of great concerns of this description; and that too much is not to be expected from him. The worst that can happen to him, in my opinion, is, that he should remain long in England; and if it had been arranged that he should go to the Prussian army, and his father had not been in London, I should have advised him on his departure to stay in London as short a time as was possible, and to keep himself quite clear of cabals and disputes, and I am sure he would have done as I should desire him.   His father being there, things are different; and as he is looked to as the head of the insurrection in Holland, he will have to wait in London, of course, till there shall be some appearance of such an insurrection. (*To Earl Bathurst.   Freueda*, 18*th May*, 1813.)

VITTORIA.

I have the pleasure to inform you that we beat the French army commanded by the King, in a general action near Vittoria yesterday, having taken from them more than 120 pieces of cannon, all their ammunition, baggage, provisions, money, &c.   Our loss has not been severe. . . . I am much concerned to add to this account that of the severe wound and reported death of Cadogan. . . . He had distinguished himself early in the action; . . . and received a wound in the spine, as I am informed, and he died last night. . . . His private character and his worth as an individual were not greater than his merits as an officer, and I shall ever regret him.   The concern which I feel upon his loss has diminished exceedingly the satisfaction I should derive from our success, as it will yours. (*Salvatierra*, 22*nd June*, 1813.)

PUBLIC TRADUCERS.

. . . All those who serve the public honestly and faithfully have for their enemies and traducers those who are desirous of profiting by the public wants, inconveniences and disasters, and by the misfortunes of the times. (*To Major-Gen. Cooke. Amusco, 9th June,* 1813.)

SERVICES RENDERED TO SPAIN.

It is not my habit, nor do I feel inclined, to make a parade of my services to the Spanish nation; but I must say that I have never abused the powers with which the Government and the Cortes have entrusted me, in any, the most trifling instance, nor have ever used them for any purpose excepting to forward the public service. (*To the Minister at War, Cadiz. Huarle, 2nd July,* 1813.)

LITTLE REAL DISCIPLINE IN THE ARMY.

The fact is that if discipline means habits of obedience to orders, as well as military instruction, we have but little of it in the army. Nobody ever thinks of obeying an order; and all the regulations of the Horse Guards, as well as of the War Office, and all the orders of the army applicable to this peculiar service are so much waste paper.

It is, however, an unrivalled army for fighting, if the soldiers can only be kept in their ranks during the battle; but it wants some of those qualities which are indispensable, to enable a General to bring them into the field in the order in which an army ought to be to meet an enemy, or to take all the advantage to be derived from a victory; and the cause of these defects is the want of habits of obedience and attention to orders by the inferior officers, and, indeed, I might add, by all. They never attend to an order with an intention to obey it, or sufficiently to understand it be it ever so clear, and therefore never obey it when obedience becomes troublesome, or difficult or important. (*To Col. Torrens, Military Secretary. Lesaca,* 18*th July,* 1813.)

The Great Want of the Nation.

The great want of this nation is of men capable of conducting public business of any description; and the Revolution, as it is called, instead of having caused an improvement in this respect, has rather augmented the evil by bringing forward into public employment of importance more inexperienced people, and by giving to men in general false notions, entirely incompatible with the nature of their business; then all real improvements in the mode of governing and of transacting business are despised by the Government and Cortes, and never thought of. (*To Lieut.-Gen. Lord W. Bentinck. Lesaca, 20th July,* 1813.)

The Spanish Character.

Your Lordship must have seen enough of the Spanish character, during the contest and our connection with them, to be aware that it will not answer to press any measure upon them which they don't like. I have not seen amongst them the slightest inclination to employ English officers to discipline their troops to such an extent as would answer any useful purpose; and I believe that one of the reasons for which they like me so well is, that, contrary to their expectations, I have not pressed them to take English officers. Besides, as I have above stated to your Lordship, the Spanish troops don't want discipline, if by discipline is meant instruction, so much as they do a system of order, which can be founded only on regular pay and food, and good care and clothing. These British officers could not give them; and notwithstanding that the Portuguese are now the *fighting-cocks* of the army, I believe we owe their merits more to the care we have taken of their pockets and bellies than to the instruction we have given them. In the end of last campaign, they behaved, in many instances, exceedingly ill, because they were in extreme misery, the Portuguese government having neglected to pay them. I have forced the Portuguese government to make arrangements to pay them regularly this year, and everybody knows how they behave. Our own troops always fight, but the influence of regular pay is seriously felt on their conduct, their health, and their efficiency; and as for the French troops, it is notorious that they will do nothing unless regularly paid and fed. (*To the Earl of Liverpool. Lesaca, 25th July,* 1813.)

"BLUDGEON WORK" AT LESACA.

I never saw such fighting as we have had here. It began on the 25th, and excepting the 29th, when not a shot was fired, we had it every day till the 2nd. The battle of the 28th was fair *bludgeon* work. The 4th division was principally engaged; and the loss of the enemy was immense. Our loss has likewise been very severe, but not of a nature to cripple us. (*To Lieut.-General Lord W. Bentinck, K.B. Lesaca, 5th Aug.* 1813.)

LANGUAGE OF OFFICERS.

It has always been my wish, as your Excellency knows, to support the existing authority; and there are not wanting instances, since I have held the command of the Spanish army, of my having interposed to prevent officers in high stations from assuming authority not belonging to them, and from using language in their addresses to be laid before the Government more expressive of their irritated feelings than of their respect. Such conduct and language is, in ordinary circumstances, quite inexcusable. And the only excuse which can be alleged for its existence (which is none for its continuance) is the state in which the Government and army of Spain had been for some time past. (*To the Minister of War, Cadiz. Lesaca, 7th Aug.* 1813.)

LIMITS TO MILITARY SUCCESS.

It is a very common error, among those unacquainted with military affairs, to believe that there are no limits to military success. . . . An army which has made such marches, and has fought such battles, as that under my command has, is necessarily much deteriorated. Independently of the actual loss of numbers by death, wounds, and sickness, many men and officers are out of the ranks for various causes. The equipment of the army, their ammunition, the soldiers' shoes, &c., require renewal; the magazines for the new operations require to be collected and formed; and many arrangements to be made without which the army could not exist a day, but which are not generally understood by those who have not had the direction of such concerns in their hands. Then observe that this new operation is the invasion of France, in which country everybody is a soldier, where the whole population is armed and organized, under persons, not as in other countries inexperienced in arms, but men who in the course of the last twenty-five years, in which France has been engaged in war with all Europe, must, the majority of them at least, have served somewhere. (*To Earl Bathurst. Lesaca, 8th Aug.* 1813.)

HOW THE POWER OF THE WORLD IS TO BE RESTORED.

The object of each [country] should be to diminish the power and influence of France, by which alone the peace of the world can be restored and maintained; and although the aggrandizement and security of the power of one's own country is the duty of every man, all nations may depend upon it, that the best security for power and for every advantage now possessed or to be acquired, is to be found in the reduction of the power and influence of the grand disturber; and in the adoption of some scheme for that object, to be acted upon by the allies in concert, whether in the negotiation for peace, or in the operations of war. (*To Earl Bathurst. Lesaca,* 14th *Aug.* 1813)

The Use of Mortars in a Siege.

I am quite certain that the use of mortars and howitzers in a siege for the purpose of what —— —— calls *general annoyance,* answers no purpose whatever, against a Spanish place occupied by the French troops, excepting against the inhabitants of the place; and eventually, when we shall get the place, against ourselves, and the convenience we should derive from having the houses of the place in a perfect state of repair. (*To Lieut.-Gen. Sir T. Graham, K.B. Lesaca,* 23rd *Aug.* 1813.)

Not tired of Success.

Your lordship may depend upon it that I am by no means tired of success; and that I shall do everything in my power to draw the attention of the enemy to this quarter, as soon as I shall know that hostilities are really renewed in Germany. (*To Earl Bathurst. Lesaca,* 23rd *Aug.* 1813.)

Spanish Slavery.

If the Princess (of Brazil) is to be a Regent according to the Constitution, the British Government need not feel much anxiety respecting her feelings or her conduct. She will be the slave of the Cortes, as all the other Regents have been and must be, so long as matters continue as they are ; and the Cortes will continue to be the slaves of the mob of the place of their residence, and of their leaders the writers of the newspapers, as all such assemblies, particularly of Spaniards, must be. (*To Earl Bathurst. Lesaca, 5th Sept.* 1813.)

Promotion by Interest.

. . . I have never interfered directly to procure for any officer serving under my command, those marks of his Majesty's favour by which many have been honoured; nor do I believe that any have ever applied for them, or have hinted through any other quarter their desire to obtain them. They have been conferred, as far as I have any knowledge, spontaneously, in the only mode in my opinion in which favours can be acceptable, or honours and distinctions can be received with satisfaction. The only share which I have had in these transactions has been by bringing the merits and services of the several officers of the army distinctly under the view of the Sovereign and the public, in my reports to the Secretary of State ; and I am happy to state that no general in this army has more frequently than yourself deserved and obtained this favourable report of your services and conduct. It is impossible for me even to guess what are the shades of distinction by which those are guided who advise the Prince Regent in the bestowing those honourable marks of distinction, and you will not expect that I should enter upon such a discussion. What I would recommend to you is to express neither disappointment nor wishes upon the subject, even to an intimate friend, much less to the Government. Continue as you have done hitherto to deserve the honourable distinction to which you aspire, and you may be certain that if the Government is wise you will obtain it. If you should not obtain it, you may depend upon it that there is no person of whose good opinion you would be solicitous who will think the worse of you on that account. . . . Notwithstanding the numerous favours that I have received from the Crown I have never solicited one, and I have never hinted, nor would any one of my friends or relations venture to hint for me, a desire to receive even one; and much as I have been favoured, the consciousness that it has been spontaneously by the King and Regent gives me more satisfaction than anything else. I recommend to you the same conduct and patience, and above all, resignation, if, after all, you should not succeed in acquiring what you wish, and I beg you to recall your letters, which you may be certain will be of no use to you. (*To* ———. *Lesaca,* 10th *Sept.* 1813.)

Best Method of Recruiting.

I entirely concur with you in thinking that the best measure you can adopt to aid the recruiting of the army is to give an allowance to the wives and children, particularly of the Irish and Scotch soldiers. When I was in office, in Ireland, I had an opportunity of knowing that the women took the utmost pains to prevent the men from volunteering to serve in the line, and from enlisting, naturally enough, because from that moment they went, not upon the parish, but upon the dunghill to starve. Indeed it is astonishing that any Irish militia soldier was ever found to volunteer; they must be certainly the very worst members of society, and I have often been induced to attribute the frequency and enormity of the crimes committed by the soldiers to our having so many men who must have left their families to starve for the inducement of a few guineas to get drunk. A provision, however, for the wives and children of the soldiers will probably revive the spirit of volunteering, and we shall get better men than we have at present. (*To Earl Bathurst. Lesaca,* 24*th Sept.* 1813.)

Plunder of St. Sebastian.

In regard to the plunder of the town (San Sebastian) by the soldiers, I am the last man who will deny it, because I know that it is true. It has fallen to my lot to take many towns by storm, and I am concerned to add, that I never saw or heard of one so taken by any troops that it was not plundered. It is one of the evil consequences attending the necessity of storming a town, which every officer laments, not only on account of the evil thereby inflicted on the unfortunate inhabitants, but on account of the injury it does to discipline, and the risk which is incurred of the loss of all the advantages of victory, at the very moment they are gained. . . . Notwithstanding that I am convinced it is impossible to prevent a town in such a situation from being plundered, I can prove that upon this occasion, particular pains were taken to prevent it. I gave most positive orders upon the subject, and desired that the officers might be warned of the peculiar situation of the place, the garrison having the castle to retire to, and of the danger that they would attempt to retake the town if they found the assailants were engaged in plunder. (*To the Right Hon. Sir H. Wellesley, K.B. Lesaca,* 9*th Oct.* 1813.)

Newspaper Harm.

Our newspapers do us plenty of harm by that which they insert, but I never suspected that they could do us the injury of alienating us from a government and nation

with which on every account we ought to be on the best
of terms, by that which they omit. I who have been
in public life in England, know well that there is nothing
more different from a debate in Parliament than the
representation of that debate in the newspapers. The
fault which I find with our newspapers is, that they so
seldom state an event or transaction as it really occurred
(unless when they absolutely copy what is written for
them), and their observations wander so far from the
text even when they have a dispatch or other writing
before them that they appear to be absolutely incapable
of understanding, much less of stating the truth on any
subject. (*To His Excellency Sir C. Stuart, K.B. Vera,*
11*th Oct.* 1813.)

LIBEL.

. . . I never saw such a libel as in the *Duende.*
If it is published in England I shall prosecute the printer.
. . . I don't know how long my temper will last, but
I was never so much disgusted with anything as with
this libel, and I don't know whether the conduct of the
soldiers in plundering San Sebastian, or the libels of the
Xefe Politico and *Duende* made me most angry. (*To
the Right Hon. Sir H. Wellesley, K.B. Vera,* 11*th Oct.*
1813.)

A SHOWER OF CALUMNIES.

There is no end of the calumnies against me and the
army, and I should have no time to do anything else, if
I were to begin either to refute or even to notice them.
Very lately they took the occasion of a libel in an *Irish*
newspaper, reporting a supposed conversation between
Castaños and me (in which I am supposed to have consented to change my religion to become King of Spain,

and he to have promised the consent of the grandees), to accuse me of this intention; and then those fools, the Duques de —— and de * * *, and the Viscomte de ——, protest formally that they are not of the number of the grandees who had given their consent to such an arrangement ! ! ! What can be done with such libels and such people, excepting despise them, and continuing one's road without noticing them?

I should have taken no notice of the libel about San Sebastian if it had not come officially before me in the letter from the Minister at War; nor shall I of this second libel in the *Duende*, although, from what I see of it in the *Redactor*, for I don't take the *Duende*, it is obvious that it comes from the Minister at War; and is written in expectation that my answer to his letter would be, that there had been no plunder and no punishment. (*To the Right Hon. Sir H. Wellesley, K.B. Vera, 16th Oct. 1813.*)

The Medal Question.

In regard to the medals I have always been of opinion that Government should have extended the principle more than they did; and in executing their orders, I believe it will be found that whenever a medal could be given to an individual under the orders of government, I have inserted his name in the return. However, my decision on this or any other subject is not final; and if anybody doubts I wish he would apply to a superior authority. . . .

In regard to the Ciudad Rodrigo medal, it is for the storm of the place. Those officers and troops even employed in the siege don't get it; much less the larger part of the army brought there to protect the operation of the siege in case of necessity. . . However, my judgment or fairness must not be relied on in these cases; and I can have no objection to an appeal from it, to higher authority on any point. (*To Marshal Sir W. C. Beresford, K.B. Vera, 6th Nov.* 1813.)

GERMAN TROOPS.

Although I am very well pleased with the German troops (and in one respect, their health, they are very superior to any you could send us), they desert so terribly, and in this respect set our men so bad an example, that I should not be sorry to get rid of them. It is really quite disgraceful. I don't believe a man remains of the last recruits sent out to the German Legion. They were raised from the prisoners sent home after the battle of Vittoria, and I would observe that if this is to be allowed it would be much better to enlist them here, as Government would at least save the expense of their passage to England and back. They generally belong to the Nassau regiment, which we are endeavouring to bring over in a body, and in the meantime are recruiting it in detail. Between the Spaniards, Germans, and I am sorry to add English, I believe we have not lost less than 1,200 men in the last four months. The Portuguese (to their honour be it recollected) do not desert to the enemy; when they go, it is to return to their own country. (*To Earl Bathurst. Vera, 9th Nov.* 1813.)

BUONAPARTE AND THE FRENCH.

I have had a good deal of conversation with people here and at St. Pé, regarding the sentiments of the people of France in general respecting Buonaparte and his Government; and I have found it to be exactly what might be supposed from all that we have heard and know

G

of his system. They all agree in one opinion, viz. that the sentiment throughout France is the same as I have found it here, an earnest desire to get rid of him, from a conviction that as long as he governs, they will have no peace. The language common to all is, that although the grievous hardships and oppression under which they suffer are intolerable, they dare not have the satisfaction even of complaining ; that on the contrary they are obliged to pretend to rejoice, and that they are allowed only to lament in secret and in silence their hard fate. . . . I can only tell you that if I were a Prince of the House of Bourbon, nothing should prevent me from now coming forward, not in a good house in London, but in the field in France ; and if Great Britain would stand by him I am sure he would succeed. This success would be much more certain in a month or more hence when Napoleon commences to carry into execution the oppressive measures which he must adopt in order to try to retrieve his fortunes. . . .

I am convinced more than ever that Napoleon's power stands upon corruption, that he has no adherents in France but the principal officers of his army, and the *employés civils* of the Government, and possibly some of the new proprietors ; but even these last I consider doubtful. Notwithstanding this state of things I recommend to your lordship to make peace with him if you can acquire all the objects which you have a right to expect. All the powers of Europe require peace possibly more than France ; and it would not do to found a new system of war upon the speculations of any individual on what he sees and learns in one corner of France. If Buonaparte becomes moderate, he is probably as good a sovereign as we can desire in France, if he does not we shall have another war in a few years, but if my speculations are well founded we shall have all France against him ; time will have been given for the supposed disaffection to his Government to produce its effect; his diminished resources will have decreased his means of corruption, and it may be hoped that he will be engaged single-handed against insurgent France and all Europe. (*To Earl Bathurst. St. Jean de Luz*, 21*st Nov.* 1813.)

Military Impossibilities.

In military operations there are some things which cannot be done; one of these is to move troops in this country during or immediately after a violent fall of rain . . .

Another observation which I have to submit is, that in a war in which every day offers a crisis, the result of which may affect the world for ages, the change of the scene of the operations of the British army would put that army entirely *hors de combat* for four months at least, even if the new scene were Holland; and they would not then be such a machine as this army is . . .

Then I beg you to observe, that whenever you extend your assistance to any country, unless at the same time fresh means are put in action, the service is necessarily stinted in all its branches on the old stage. (*To Earl Bathurst. St. Jean de Luz,* 21*st Dec.* 1813.)

Desire of the French to rid themselves of Napoleon.

Every day's experience here shows the desire of the people to shake off the yoke of Napoleon. It is a curious circumstance that we are the protectors of the property of the inhabitants against the plunder of their own armies, and their cattle, property, &c., are driven into our lines for protection. (*To Earl Bathurst. St. Jean de Luz,* 1*st Jan.* 1814.)

DETESTATION OF BUONAPARTE.

. . . We have found the French people exactly what we might expect (not from the lying accounts in the French newspapers, copied into all the others of the world, and believed by everybody, notwithstanding the internal sense of every man of their falsehood, but) from what we knew of the Government of Napoleon, and the oppression of all descriptions under which his subjects have laboured. It is not easy to describe the detestation of this man. What do you think of the French people running into our posts for protection from the French troops with their bundles on their heads, and their *beds*, as you recollect to have seen the people of Portugal and Spain. (*To Lord Burghersh. St. Jean de Luz*, 14*th Jan.* 1814.)

CONTAGION.

I have known many instances of contagion in military hospitals, which have not affected in some instances more than the room or ward in which it prevailed, and seldom extended beyond the building; and I never heard before of an hospital placed in quarantine only because a few soldiers in it had a yellow appearance in their countenance.   (*To the Right Hon. Sir H. Wellesley, K.B. St. Jean de Luz,* 19*th Jan.* 1814.)

PRESERVATION OF PUBLIC HEALTH.

I don't object to any law which has for its object the preservation of the public health, but I believe it will be admitted that those charged with the execution of those laws are required to proceed with discretion ; that they ought not to create the alarm, inconvenience, confusion, and evil which have been the consequence of the measures of the *Ayuntamiento* of Santander upon this occasion without due ground ; and that they are responsible for their conduct. I can prove that there was not the slightest ground for the measure the *Ayuntamiento* of Santander adopted ; and that so far from the military commandant of the hospitals, and the medical gentlemen concurring in its necessity, the first intimation they received of it was to find themselves in quarantine under the guard of the Spanish soldiers of the garrison. (*To the Minister at War. Madrid, St. Jean de Luz,* 23rd *Jan.* 1814.)

THE NAVIGATION OF THE LAKES.

I believe that the defence of Canada, and the cooperation of the Indians, depend upon the navigation of the lakes ; and I see that both Sir G. Prevost and Commodore Barclay complain of the want of the crews of two sloops of war. Any offensive operation founded upon Canada must be preceded by the establishment of a naval superiority on the lakes...

The prospect in regard to America is not consoling. That power will always hang on the skirts of Great Britain unless there should be some change in her own situation ; or the state of the Spanish colonies should make an alteration, not only in America in general but in the colonial system of the world ; or our own colonies in America should grow so fast, as that with very little assistance from the mother country, they shall be equal to their own defence. (*To Earl Bathurst. Garris,* 22nd *Feb.* 1814.)

THE TWO DYNASTIES.

I write just one line to let you know that in proportion as we advance, I find the sentiment in the country still more strong against the Buonaparte dynasty, and in favour of the Bourbons; but I am quite certain there will be no declaration on the part of the people, if the allies do not in some manner declare themselves, or at all events, as long as they are negotiating with Buona-parte any declaration from us would, I am convinced, raise such a flame in the country as would soon spread from one end of it to the other, and would infallibly over-turn him.

I cannot discover the policy of not hitting one's enemy as hard as one can, and in the most vulnerable place. I am certain that he would not so act by us if he had the opportunity. He would certainly overturn British au-thority in Ireland if it were in his power. (*To the Earl of Liverpool. St. Sevec, 4th March,* 1814.)

Evils inseparable from War.

What has occurred in the last six years in the Penin-sula should be an example to all military men on this point, and should induce them to take especial care to endeavour to conciliate the country which is the seat of war, by preserving the most strict discipline among the troops, by mitigating as much as possible the evils which are inseparable from war, and by that demeanour in the officers in particular towards the inhabitants which will show them that they at least do not encourage the evils which they suffer from the soldiers, and will afford the inhabitants some hope that the evils will be redressed and will be of short duration.

All soldiers are inclined to plunder, and can be pre-vented only by the constant attention and exertion of the officers; and I earnestly entreat you to urge those of the army under your command to attend to these circumstances. (*To Gen. Dom. M. Freyre. St. Sevec,* 5th March, 1814.)

The Bourbon Party.

There is a large party at Bordeaux in favour of the House of Bourbon, and I beg you to adhere to the following instructions in regard to this party and their views.

If they should ask for your consent to proclaim Louis XVIII., to hoist the white standard, &c., you will state that the British nation and their allies wish well to Louis XVIII.; and as long as the public peace is preserved where our troops are stationed, we shall not interfere to prevent that party from doing what may be deemed most for its interest; nay further, that I am prepared to assist any party that may show itself inclined to aid us in getting the better of Buonaparte.

That the object of the allies in the war, however, and above all, in entering France, is as stated in my proclamation, *Peace;* and that it is well known the allies are now engaged in negotiating a treaty of peace with Buonaparte. That however I might be inclined to aid and support any set of people against Buonaparte while at war, I could give them no further aid when peace should be concluded; and I beg the inhabitants will weigh this matter well before they raise a standard against the Government of Buonaparte, and involve themselves in hostilities.

If, however, notwithstanding this warning, the town should think proper to hoist the white standard, and should proclaim Louis XVIII., or adopt any other measure of that description, you will not oppose them, and you will arrange with the authorities the means of drawing without loss of time for all the arms, ammunition, &c., which are at Dax, which you will deliver to them.

If the municipality should state that they will not proclaim Louis XVIII. without your orders, you will decline to give such orders for the reasons above stated. (*To Marshal Sir W. C. Beresford, K.B. St. Sevec, 7th March,* 1814.)

MARSHAL SOULT.

We beat Marshal Soult completely on the 27th February, near Orthez. His loss was immense in the action, and has been greater since by the general desertion of his troops. We pursued after the battle, and crossed the Adour at this place on the 1st, but on that evening a violent storm came on, which filled all the rivers and torrents, carried away our bridges of pontoons, cut off all our communications for the movement of our troops, supplies, &c., and I have been obliged to halt to remedy the evil. In the meantime I have detached Marshal Beresford with a considerable corps towards Bordeaux, and I intend myself to follow the movements of the enemy with the great body of the army towards Auch.

I find the whole population in this part of the country decidedly hostile to Buonaparte's Government, and generally desirous for the restoration of the Bourbon family; and I am quite certain that if the allies were to declare in their favour there is not a soul in this part of France who would not rise in the cause. (*To Lieut.-Col. Lord Burghersh, St. Sevec, 8th March,* 1814.)

KING JOSEPH'S BAGGAGE.

The baggage of King Joseph, after the battle of Vittoria, fell into my hands, after having been plundered by the soldiers; and I found among it an imperial containing prints, drawings, and pictures.

From the cursory view which I took of them, the latter did not appear to me to be anything remarkable.

There are certainly not among them any of the fine pictures which I saw in Madrid by Raffaele and others; and I thought more of the prints and drawings, all of the Italian school, which induced me to believe that the whole collection was robbed in Italy, rather than in Spain. I sent them to England, and having desired that they should be put to rights, and those cleaned which required it, I have found that there are among them much finer pictures than I conceived there were, and as if the King's palaces have been robbed of pictures, it is not improbable that some of his may be among them, and I am desirous of restoring them to his Majesty, I shall be much obliged to you if you will mention the subject to Don J. Luyando, and tell him that I request that a person may be sent to London to see them, and to fix upon those belonging to his Majesty. (*To the Right Hon. Sir H. Wellesley, K.B. Aire, 16th March,* 1814.)

The Head of the Army.

I am not acting as an individual, I am at the head of the army, and the confidential agent of three independent nations; and supposing that as an individual I could submit to have my views and intentions in such a case misrepresented, as the general of the allied army I cannot. (*To H.R.H. the Duc d'Angoulème. Seysses,* 29*th March,* 1814.)

False Reports.

You are quite right to put no faith in reports from the coast of France. There are more false reports in France than even in Spain. In fact between the Government, and those who detest the Government, there is no truth in France. I have been told twenty times that

Buonaparte was dead, that he had died of a wound, was poisoned, was dead of the gravel, &c., &c., that the Congress was dissolved, that there was an insurrection in La Vendée, in Brittany, &c., &c., the whole being false. (*To Col. Bunbury, Under Secretary of State. Seysses, 1st April,* 1814.)

Vittoria Medals.

I have received your letter of the 16th March, regarding the recommendation for the medals for the battle of Vittoria. I make a distinction between a general action in which we pursue the enemy from the ground, and one in a defensive position. This distinction is fairly deducible from the different nature of the operations.

In the former it is very difficult to tell who is and who is not engaged in musketry. All are at times to a certain degree exposed to it; and I perfectly recollect seeing the Household Brigade at one time in a situation in the pursuit in which they were so. In an action in a defensive position there are always some troops so situated as to have no share whatever in the action; some may be at the distance of miles from it, and in those cases I apply the rule strictly. In actions such as Salamanca and Vittoria I don't. (*To Col. Torrens, Military Secretary. Seysses, 1st April,* 1814.)

Peace the Object of the Government.

The object of the Governments that I have the honour to serve has always been peace, a peace founded upon the independence of their respective states, and that of the rest of the European Powers, and I have every reason to believe that the ambassadors of these august Sovereigns are at present engaged in concert with their allies of the North of Europe, at Châtillon sur Seine, in negotiating such a peace, if it is possible to obtain it with the existing Government of France (Translation). (*To the Municipality of Toulouse. Toulouse,* 12*th April,* 1814.)

THE BATTLE OF TOULOUSE.

The question is then discussed, who won the battle of Toulouse? . . .

The battle was fought on the 10th of April; it ended by the allied army being in possession of all the works on Mount Celoinet, and (with the exception of the Faubourg Guillemeire, and its fortified posts at Sucarin and Cambon) of all the ground on the right of the Canal de Languedoc, and their posts of cavalry on the bridges of the canal above the town.

On the 11th of April, Marshal Soult wrote a letter to the Ministre de la Guerre, and to Marshal Suchet, in which he clearly indicated what must be the result of the previous day's battle. He states the probability of his retiring from Toulouse. On the same day he made all the preparations, arrangements and dispositions for the retreat which was made on that night. . .

M. Choumara contends that Marshal Soult, having remained in Toulouse for twenty-four hours after the battle, won the battle of Toulouse, as the allies had in 1810 won the battle of Busaco, their position having been turned by Marshal Massena after his army had been repulsed, and the allies having abandoned Coimbra. There is this difference in the two cases. The battle of Busaco was fought fifteen miles from Coimbra. The French army gained no part of the position of the allies in the battle of Busaco, not even a *mamelon.* They were totally and entirely defeated and repulsed at all points. The result of the battle gave Marshal Massena no facility in making his subsequent movement to turn the position of the allies. In the battle of Toulouse the allies carried, after a most desperate struggle, the key of the fortified position of the French army; the most important point in it, according to the opinion of Marshal Soult, the Commander-in-Chief of the allies, and every officer concerned on either side. They held undisturbed possession of this position. From their ground they could by their fire prevent the occupation of the remainder of the position of their enemy. The possession of it gave them the means of which advantage was taken to cut off the retreat of their enemy; and their advanced troops were actually on the night of the 11th on the ground over which Marshal Soult was under the necessity of passing on the same night in his retreat. Marshal Soult left in Toulouse about 1,600 prisoners, three general officers, and several pieces of cannon. None were in Coimbra in 1810 after Busaco. But there is another remarkable difference between the affairs at Toulouse and at Busaco. The French army left at Coimbra, when they passed that town after the battle, not less than 6,000 sick and wounded, who were captured in the town in little more than a week by Gen. Trant. The battle of Toulouse had no resemblance to the battle of Busaco. M. Choumara's readers will judge which party won it. (*Extracts from Memoranda on* "*Considerations Militaires sur les Mémoires du Maréchal Suchet, et sur la Bataille de Toulouse: par S. Choumara, ancien capitaine du Génie.*"

BUONAPARTE OVERTURNED.

Upon my entrance into Toulouse on the 12th inst. I found the statues of Buonaparte overturned, and the white flag flying, and everybody wearing the white cockade. (*To the Minister at War, Madrid. Toulouse, 14th April*, 1814.)

CRAMPED BY INSTRUCTIONS.

In regard to my proceedings here I was bound by my instructions, and cramped by the total ignorance in which I was of the state of the negotiations at Châtillon. You in England gallop very fast, and you think that everything ought to go on as it appears to you. You forget, however, now and then that your officers are very strictly instructed, and that those who mean to serve their country well must obey their instructions, however fearless they may be of responsibility. Indeed I attribute this fearlessness very much to the determination never to disobey, as long as the circumstances exist under which an order is given. (*To E. Cooke, Esq., Under Secretary of State. Toulouse*, 16th *April*, 1814.)

THE SLAVE TRADE.

I was not aware till I had been here some time, of the degree of frenzy existing here about the slave trade, and I am unable to describe it to you. People in general appear to think that it would suit the policy of the nation to go to war to put an end to that *abominable* traffic, and many wish that we should take the field on this new crusade. All agree that no favour can be shown to a slave-trading country ; and as Spain next to Portugal is supposed to be the country which gives most protection to this trade, the interests and wishes of Spain are but little attended to here. Besides, it is not easy to describe the unpopularity attached to the king's name, from the occurrences at his return to Madrid. The newspapers afford some specimen of it,

but at a late dinner at Guildhall I recommended to the
Lord Mayor to drink the King of Spain's health, and
he told me that he was become so unpopular in the city,
he was afraid that if the toast were not positively refused it would at least be received with so much disgust
as to render it very disagreeable to me, and to every
well wisher to the Spanish Government. (*To the Right
Hon. Sir H. Wellesley, K.B. London*, 20*th July*, 1814.)

THE SLAVE TRADE.

You do me justice in believing that I will pursue
with all the zeal of which I am capable, the object of
the abolition of the slave trade by France.   .   .   .
There are but few persons now in France who have
turned their attention to the slave trade, and those
few are proprietors in the colonies, or speculators in
the trade, and interested in carrying it on.   I am sorry
to say that there is a very large interest of the former
in the House of Peers ; and it is not easy to believe
what an influence the proprietors of St. Domingo have
on all the measures of the Government.   The proposition to abolish the slave trade is foolishly enough connected with other recollections of the revolutionary
days of 1789 and 1790, and is generally unpopular.   It
is not believed that we are in earnest about it, or have
abolished the trade on the score of its inhumanity.   It
is thought to have been a commercial speculation, and
by some to have been occasioned by the Continental
system ; and that having abolished the trade ourselves,
with a view to prevent the undue increase of colonial
produce in our stores, of which we could not dispose,
we now want to prevent other nations from cultivating
their colonies to the utmost of their power. (*To W.
Wilberforce, Esq., M.P.   Paris*, 15*th Sept.* 1814.)

Fortified Places.

The operations of the revolutionary war have tended in some degree to put strong places out of fashion; and an opinion prevails which has been a good deal confirmed by the operations of the last campaign, that strong places are but little useful, and at all events are not worth the expense which they cost. Much may be urged against these new doctrines as applicable to any theatre of war, but in respect to that under discussion, it is only necessary to remind those who are to consider and decide upon the subject that in the war of the revolution the whole of the Austrian Netherlands and the Pays de Liege, from the French frontiers to the Meuse, those very provinces fell into the hands of the enemy in consequence of one unsuccessful battle, of no very great importance in itself, fought near Mons; that the allies regained them with equal rapidity in the following campaign, when they had a superiority of force; and that, very imperfect field works only having been thrown up at some points during the period of their possession by the allies, the enemy did not find it so easy as they had before, and it required much more time to get possession of the country, when the enemy regained the superiority of force in the year 1794, notwithstanding that that superiority was much more commanding than it had been in November, 1792. (*Extract from Memorandum on the defence of the frontier of the Netherlands. Paris, 22nd Sept. 1814.*)

The Slavery Question.

You judge most correctly regarding the state of the public mind here upon this question (abolition of slavery). Not only is there no information, but because

England takes an interest in the question, it is impossible to convey any through the only channel which would be at all effectual, viz. the daily press. Nobody reads anything but the newspapers; but it is impossible to get anything inserted in any French newspaper in Paris in favour of the abolition, or even to show that the trade was abolished in England from motives of humanity. The extracts made from English newspapers upon this, or any other subject, are selected with a view either to turn our conduct or principles into ridicule, or to exasperate against us still more the people of this country, and therefore the evil cannot be remedied by good publications in the daily press in England with a view to their being copied into the newspapers here. . . . I must say that the daily press in England do us a good deal of harm in this as well as in other questions. We are sure of the king and his government, if he could rely upon the opinion of his people, but as long as our press teems with writings drawn with a view to irritate persons here, we shall never be able to exercise the influence which we ought to have upon this question, and which we really possess. (*To W. Wilberforce, Esq., M.P. Paris, 8th Oct.* 1814.)

French Neutrality.

The objectionable rule in the French system of neutrality is that in a war with Great Britain the privateers or ships of war of the two nations should find an asylum in a French port on any account excepting when driven here by stress of weather. The abstract principle of such a rule may be fair enough; but when applied to the situation of the two belligerents, and when it is considered that an American privateer, or ship of war, is in these seas solely for the purposes of hostility against the

British trade, and that this hostility could not be carried on if she had not this asylum in a French port, it will appear very unfair and highly disadvantageous to Great Britain. (*To Viscount Castlereagh, K.G. Paris,* 18*th Oct.* 1814.)

Newspapers and the Slave-trade.

I have had no reason to complain of the newspapers lately on the subject of the slave-trade, and I hope they will continue not to notice it for some little time longer. (*To W. Wilberforce, Esq., M.P. Paris,* 4*th Nov.* 1814.)

Buonaparte.

Buonaparte governed one half of Europe directly, and almost the other half indirectly. (*To General Dumourier. Paris,* 26*th Nov.* 1814.)

Object in Abolishing the Slave-trade.

I was yesterday told gravely by the *Directeur de la Marine* that one of our objects in abolishing the slave-trade was to get recruits to fight our battles in America! ! ! and it was hinted that a man might as well be a slave for agricultural labour as a soldier for life ; and that the difference was not worth the trouble of discussing it. (*To W. Wilberforce, Esq., M.P. Paris,* 14*th Dec.* 1814.)

Refusal to Bury Mlle. Rancourt.

The celebrated actress Mlle. Rancourt died a few days ago, and her fellow comedians determined to bury her at St. Roch, and proceeded thither in a body, attended by an immense mob, on Tuesday. The actors of the Théâtre Français having been excommunicated, I imagine, in the reign of Louis XV., the curate of St.

Roch refused to receive the body into the church, or to administer the usual rites; and the mob broke open the church doors, and, having introduced the body, forced the curate to perform the service.

The King in the meantime having been informed of what was passing, sent one of his chaplains, attended by some of the *Gardes du Corps*, to perform the service; and the mob, among whom had been heard the cries of " Les Prêtres à la lanterne," dispersed with the cries of " Vive le Roi." (*To Viscount Castlereagh, K.G. Paris, 19th Jan.* 1815.)

What brought Buonaparte back.

It is the desire for war, particularly in the army, that has brought Buonaparte back, and has formed for him any party, and has given him any success, and all my observations when at Paris convinced me that it was the King alone who kept Europe at peace, and that the danger which most immediately threatened his Majesty was to be attributed to his desire to maintain the peace contrary to the wishes not only of the army but of the majority of his subjects, of some of his ministers, and even of some of his family. (*To Viscount Castlereagh, K.G. Vienna, 26th March,* 1815.)

A surprising Application.

I have had the honour of receiving your letter of the 28th April, applying *to me* to be employed with this army, which, considering that you are at the Horse Guards, has not a little surprised me.

If you will speak to Sir H. Torrens, he will tell you that I have nothing to say to any appointment to the staff of this army of any rank.

However flattered I may be, and however I may applaud the desire of an officer to serve under my command in the field, it is impossible for me to recommend officers for employment with whose merits I am not acquainted, in preference to those to whose services I am so much indebted, particularly if the latter desire to serve again. But, as I before stated, I have no choice, and I beg you to apply in the quarter in which you will certainly succeed, without reference to my wishes, whenever there shall be a command vacant for you, which there is not at present. (*To Major-General Darling. Bruxelles,* 2nd *May,* 1815.)

ATTACKING THE ABSENT IN PARLIAMENT.

. . The mode of attacking a servant of the public absent on public business, day after day, in speeches in Parliament, which has lately been adopted by —— ——, appears to me most extraordinary and unprecedented.

If I have done anything wrong or unbecoming my own character, or that of the station I filled, I ought to be prosecuted or at least censured for it, in consequence of a specific motion on the subject; but it is not fair to give to the act of any individual a construction it will not fairly bear, a construction which no man breathing believes it was intended to bear; and to charge him home with being an assassin, day after day in speeches, and never in form.

I say first, that the Declaration has never been accurately translated; and the meaning of the words *vindicte publique* is not "public vengeance," but "public justice." But even if the meaning was "public vengeance," the Declaration does not deliver Buonaparte over to the dagger of the assassin. When did the dagger of the assassin execute the vengeance of the public?

In regard to his being declared " hors le loi ;" first, it must be recollected at what period and under what circumstances he was so declared. The period was the 13th of March, and although we knew Buonaparte had landed and had made progress in France sufficient to create a contest there, we were not aware that he could be established without firing a shot. The object then of this part of the publication was to strengthen the hands of the King of France by the opinion of the Congress.

Secondly, was he not " hors la loi ?" and had he or not broken all the ties which connected him with the world ? The only treaty by which he was connected with the world, was that at Fontainebleau ; that he broke.

Having quitted his asylum he landed in France with such a force as showed that he relied solely upon treachery and rebellion, not only for success but for safety. He incurred all risks in order to gain the greatest prize in Europe, one which he had abandoned only ten months before under a treaty with the Allied Powers ; and is it possible that it can be gravely asserted that Buonaparte, an individual like any other, should have been guilty by this act of only a breach of treaty ? If he was guilty of more, of which there can be no doubt, it was of the crime of rebellion and treason, with a view to usurp the sovereign authority of France; a crime which has always been deemed "hors la loi" so far as this, that all sovereigns have in all times called upon their subjects to raise their arms to protect them from him who was guilty of it. The Declaration does no more. This is my reasoning upon the subject. . . . I never knew any paper so discussed as the Declaration was ; and I believe there never was a public paper so successful, particularly in Italy and France. (*To the Right Hon. W. Wellesley Pole. Bruxelles, 5th May,* 1815.)

REFUSAL TO GRANT MATERIALS FOR A HISTORY OF THE WAR.

I return Sir W. Stewart's letter of the 13th April. I perfectly recollect the letter to which he refers. It appeared to me to be written in the anguish of mind occasioned by the loss he had sustained in his action, and by his own sufferings, and that it did not do justice to himself or to his troops; and I did not send it home or communicate it to anybody, I believe, certainly not to Mr. Philippart or to any other person calling himself an author. Indeed, I have invariably refused to communicate to any person documents to enable him to write a history of the late war; as I consider the transactions too recent for any person to write a true history, without hurting the feelings of nations and of some individuals. (*To Lieut.-Gen. Lord Hill, G.C.B. Bruxelles, 9th May,* 1815.)

ON THE DEFENSIVE.

. . . In the situation in which we are placed at present, neither at war nor at peace, unable on that account to patrol up to the enemy and ascertain his position by view, or to act offensively upon any part of his line, it is difficult, if not impossible, to combine an operation, because there are no data on which to found any combination. All we can do is to put our troops in such a situation, as in case of a sudden attack by the enemy, to render it easy to assemble, and to provide against the chance of any being cut off from the rest. (*To H.R.H. The Prince of Orange, G.C.B. Bruxelles,* 11th *May,* 1815.)

The full Value to be given.

In no well-regulated country can the property of subjects be taken from them for less than its fair value; and if any public burden is to be borne by any country, it is best that the fiscal means of imposing it should proceed regularly from the sovereign authority, and that each individual should receive the full value of his private property from the same source. (*To His Excellency Sir C. Stuart, G.C.B. Bruxelles,* 13th *May,* 1815.)

M. de Stein's Paper.

I cannot conclude without expressing my regret that such a paper as M. de Stein's should have been produced by the Prussian Legation. In a crisis of the affairs of the world, the Powers of Europe are about to embark in a great contest; and Great Britain, interested only in a secondary degree in the crisis, that can be injured only in the injury which others will suffer, comes forward with all her resources, and not only puts forth all the strength which circumstances and her situation enable her to collect, but assists with money all the Powers of Europe, small as well as great, in proportion to their several exertions, and this at a moment of unparalleled financial difficulty, occasioned by her exertions in a similar manner, in the last years of the late war.

I should be sorry that public men in England ever became disgusted with the affairs of the Continent, and that the interest felt in its concerns should be diminished; and in this sense it is, and adverting to the impression which M. de Stein's paper has made upon my mind, that I regret that such a document was ever allowed to be brought forward. (*To the Earl of Clancarty, G.C.B. Bruxelles,* 14th *May,* 1815.)

The Foundation of Buonaparte's Power in France.

Buonaparte's power in France is founded upon the military and upon nothing else, and the military must be destroyed or appeased before the people can or rather dare speak. To work effectually against the French army in France, numerous armies are necessary. Then the people may be able to speak and act without running the risk of being effectually destroyed. (Translation.) (*To the Comte de Blacas. Bruxelles,* 16*th May,* 1815.)

The Bourbons and Peace.

I have frequently told your Highness, and every day's experience shows me that I am right, that the only chance of peace for Europe consists in the establishment in France of the legitimate Bourbons. The establishment of any other Government, whether in the person of —— —— or in a Regency in the name of young Napoleon, or in any other individual, or in a republic, must lead to the maintenance of large military establishments to the ruin of all the Governments of Europe, till it shall suit the convenience of the French Government to commence a contest which can be directed only against you, or others for whom we are interested. In this contest we shall feel the additional difficulty that those who are now on our side will then be against us, and you will again find yourself surrounded by enemies. I am convinced that the penetration of your Highness will have shown you the danger of all these schemes to the interests of the Emperor; and that you will defeat them all by firmly adhering to that line of conduct (in which you will find us likewise) which will finally lead to the establishment in France of the legitimate Government, from which alone Europe can expect any genuine peace. (*To H. H. Prince Metternich. Bruxelles*, 20*th May*, 1815.)

Procuring Intelligence.

There is a good deal of *charlatanisme* in what is called procuring intelligence, as there is in everything else. (*To Earl Bathurst. Bruxelles*, 22*nd May*, 1815.)

The Worth of the "Moniteur" Articles.

. . . It is scarcely necessary to assure your Lordship that I have not issued any proclamation or order upon any political subject whatever; and I should rather imagine that the contents of the *Moniteur* in these days, and particularly the articles proceeding from the Government, are as little worthy of credit as they have been at all former periods. The object of this system of delusion is to make an impression in France, or elsewhere, for a moment; and if that object is accomplished it is supposed that all is gained. But where the truth can be known it is quite impossible that this system can have any other effect than to render contemptible its patron. (*To Viscount Castlereagh, K.G. Bruxelles*, 23*rd May*, 1815.)

Position of the Army at Waterloo.

The position which I took up in front of Waterloo crossed the high roads from Charleroi and Nivelles, and had its right thrown back to a ravine near Merke Braine, which was occupied, and its left extended to a height above the hamlet Ter La Haye, which was likewise occupied. In front of the right centre, and near the Nivelles road, we occupied the house and gardens of

Hougoumont, which covered the return of that flank; and in front of the left centre we occupied the farm of La Haye Sainte. By our left we communicated with Marshal Prince Blucher, at Waore, through Oliami, and the marshal had promised me that in case we should be attacked, he would support me with one or more corps, as might be necessary. . . . In Lieut.-Gen. Sir T. Picton his Majesty has sustained the loss of an officer who has frequently distinguished himself in his service, and he fell gloriously, leading his division to a charge with bayonets, by which one of the most serious attacks made by the enemy on our position was repulsed. The Earl of Uxbridge, after having successfully got through this arduous day, received a wound by almost the last shot fired, which will I am afraid deprive his Majesty for some time of his services. . . . H.R.H. the Prince of Orange distinguished himself by his gallantry and conduct, till he received a wound from a musket ball through the shoulder, which obliged him to quit the field. . . .

I should not do justice to my own feelings, or to Marshal Blucher and the Prussian army, if I did not attribute the successful result of this arduous day to the cordial and timely assistance I received from them. The operation of General Bulow upon the enemy's flank was a most decisive one, and even if I had not found myself in a situation to make the attack which produced the result, it would have forced the enemy to retire if his attack should have failed, and would have prevented him from taking advantage of them if they should unfortunately have succeeded. (*To Earl Bathurst. Waterloo, 19th June*, 1815.)

DEARLY-BOUGHT GLORY.

. . . I cannot express to you the regret and sorrow with which I look around me and contemplate the loss which I have sustained, particularly in your brother. The glory resulting from such actions, so dearly bought, is no consolation to me, and I cannot suggest it as any to you and his friends; but I hope that it may be expected that this last one has been so decisive, as that no doubt remains that our exertions and our individual losses will be rewarded by the early attainment of our first object. It is then that the glory of the actions in which our friends and relations have fallen, will be some consolation for their loss. (*To the Earl of Aberdeen, K.G. Bruxelles,* 19th *June,* 1815.)

REMAINS OF THE FRENCH ARMY.

The remains of the French army have retired upon Laon. All accounts agree in stating that it is in a very wretched state, and that in addition to its losses in battle and in prisoners, it is losing vast numbers of men by desertion. The soldiers quit their regiments in parties, and return to their homes; those of the cavalry and artillery, selling their horses to the people of the country. (*To Earl Bathurst. Le Cateau,* 22nd *June,* 1815.)

NAPOLEON'S DEATH-BLOW.

. . . I may be wrong, but my opinion is, that we have given Napoleon his death-blow; from all I hear his army is totally destroyed, the men are deserting in parties, even the generals are withdrawing from him. The infantry throw away their arms, and the cavalry and artillery sell their horses to the people of the country, and desert to their homes. Allowing for much exaggeration in this account, and knowing that Buonaparte can still collect, in addition to what he has brought back with him, the 5th *corps d'armée* under Rapp, which is near Strasbourg, and the 3rd corps, which was at Waore during the battle, and has not suffered so much as the others, and probably some troops from La Vendée, I am still of opinion that he can make no head against us, *qu'il n'a qu'à se pendre;* and therefore it appears to me that your brother would derive none of the advantages from his service, and would incur all the inconveniences of it. (*To Lieut.-Gen. the Earl of Uxbridge, G.C.B. Le Cateau, 23rd June,* 1815.)

CONTINUING OPERATIONS.

I could not consider Buonaparte's abdication of a usurped power in favour of his son, and his handing over the Government provisionally to five persons named by himself, to be that description of security which the Allies had in view, which should induce them to lay down their arms, and therefore I continue my operations. All accounts concur in stating that it is impossible for the enemy to collect an army to make head against us. (*To Earl Bathurst. Joncourt, 25th June,* 1815.)

BUONAPARTE'S FATE.

General —— has been here this day to negotiate for Napoleon's passing to America, to which proposition I have answered that I have no authority. The Prussians think the Jacobins wish to give him over to me, believing that I will save his life. —— wishes to kill him ; but I have told him that I shall remonstrate, and shall insist upon his being disposed of by common accord. I have likewise said that as a private friend I advised him to have nothing to do with so foul a transaction; that he and I had acted too distinguished parts in these transactions to become executioners; and that I was determined that if the sovereigns wished to put him to death they should appoint an executioner, which should not be me. . . . I am not pleased with the King's hesitation about Peroune. I have behaved in such a manner to him that he ought to be certain I would not propose anything to him that was not for the good of the cause, which is his interest more than mine. (*To His Excellency Sir C. Stuart, G.C.B. Orvillé, 28th June,* 1815.)

A Pounding Match.

You will have heard of our battle of the 18th. Never did I see such a pounding match. Both were what the boxers call "gluttons." Napoleon did not manœuvre at all. He just moved forward in the old style in columns, and was driven off in the old style. The only difference was that he mixed cavalry with his infantry, and supported both with an enormous quantity of artillery.

I had the infantry for some time in squares, and we had the French cavalry walking about us, as if they had been our own. I never saw the British infantry behave so well. (*To Marshal Lord Beresford, G.C.B. Gonesse, 2nd July,* 1815.)

Wellington and the Commissioners.

I left the commissioners at Etrées, and went to the head-quarters at Le Plessis to give the orders for the movement of the troops in the morning, and I overtook them again in the night at Lonores. I then told them that I had considered their last question since I had seen them, and that I felt no objection to give them my opinion upon it, still as an individual; that in my opinion Europe had no hope of peace if any person excepting the King was called to the throne of France; that any person so called must be considered a usurper, whatever his rank and quality; that he must act as a usurper, and must endeavour to turn the attention of the country from the defects of his title towards war and foreign conquest; that the Powers of Europe must, in such a case, guard themselves against this evil; and that I could only assure them that, unless otherwise ordered by my Government, I would exert any influence I might possess over the Allied Sovereigns to induce them to insist upon securities for the preservation of peace, besides the treaty itself, if such an arrangement as they had stated were adopted. The commissioners replied that they perfectly understood me, and some of them added, " *Et vous avez raison.*" (*To Earl Bathurst. Gonesse, 2nd July,* 1815.)

Bad Conduct of the Allies.

You will have heard of our great battle in Flanders, and of its final result in the surrender of Buonaparte to the *Bellerophon,* off the Isle d'Aix, and if the Allies will only be a little moderate, that is, if they will prevent plunder by their troops, and take only what is necessary for their own security, we may hope for permanent peace. But I confess that I am a little afraid of them. They are all behaving exceedingly ill. (*To the Right Hon. Sir H. Wellesley, G.C.B. Paris, 19th July,* 1815.)

The Battle of Waterloo.

The battle of Waterloo was certainly the hardest fought that has been for many years, I believe, and has placed in the power of the allies the most important results. We are throwing them away, however, by the infamous conduct of some of us ; and I am sorry to add that our own Government also are taking up a little too much of the tone of their rascally newspapers. They are shifting their objects ; and having got their cake they want both to eat it and keep it. (*To Marshal Lord Beresford, G.C.B. Paris,* 7*th Aug.* 1815.)

History of a Battle compared to that of a Ball.

I have received your letter of the 2nd, regarding the battle of Waterloo. The object which you propose to yourself is very difficult of attainment, and if really attained is not a little invidious. The history of a battle is not unlike the history of a ball. Some individuals may recollect all the little events of which the great result is the battle won or lost; but no individual can recollect the order in which, or the exact moment at which they occurred, which makes all the difference as to their value or importance. Then the faults or the misbehaviour of some gave occasion for the distinction of others, and perhaps were the cause of material losses ; and you cannot write a true history of a battle without including the faults and misbehaviour of a part at least of those engaged.

Believe me, that every man you see in a military uniform is not a hero; and that, although in the account given of a general action, such as that of Waterloo, many instances of individual heroism must be passed over unrelated, it is better for the general interests to leave those parts of the story untold, than to tell the whole truth. (*To——— ———, Esq. Paris,* 8*th Aug.* 1815.)

ACCOUNTS NOT TO BE RELIED ON.

I have received your letter of the 11th, and I regret much that I have not been able to prevail upon you to relinquish your plan ; you may depend upon it you will never make it a satisfactory work. . . . . . .
Just to show you how little reliance can be placed even on what are supposed the best accounts of a battle, I mention that there are some circumstances mentioned in Gen. ———'s account which did not occur as he relates them. He was not on the field during the whole battle, particularly not during the latter part of it. . .
The battle began, I believe, at eleven. It is impossible to say when each important occurrence took place, nor in what order. . . . .
. . . Remember, I recommend you to leave the battle of Waterloo as it is. (*To* ——— ———, *Esq.* * *Paris, 17th Aug.* 1815.)

OBJECTIONS TO A GENERAL COURT MARTIAL.

I confess that I feel very strong objections to discuss before a General Court Martial the conduct of any individual in such a battle as that of Waterloo. It generally brings before the public circumstances which might as well not be published; and the effect is equally produced by obliging him who has behaved ill to withdraw from the service. (*To H. R. H. the Duke of York. Paris, 12th Sept.* 1815.)

THE POSITION OF FRANCE.

It is on many accounts desirable, as well for their own happiness as for that of the world, that the people

---

* See also letter on p. 115.

of France, if they do not already feel that Europe is too strong for them, should be made sensible of it ; and that whatever may be the extent at any time of their momentary and partial success against any one, or any number of individual powers in Europe, the day of retribution must come. (*To Viscount Castlereagh, K.G. Paris*, 23rd Sept. 1815.)

JUSTICE.

I had already heard of the letter which your Excellency has sent me from the Duc d'Otrante to the *Préfet des Bouches du Rhône.* Whatever a man may have done during a revolution which has lasted for twenty-five years, he cannot, consistently with any principle, be arrested and confined in an arbitrary manner, if it is intended to put an end to the revolution, and that the country should be governed with justice and according to law. On these grounds I cannot disapprove of the letter from the Duc d'Otrante, whatever may have been his motive for writing it. (*To Admiral Lord Exmouth, G.C.B. Paris*, 26th Sept. 1815.)

RECOLLECTIONS.

. . . I am highly gratified by your Royal Highness' expressions of your recollection of past years and events. I assure your Royal Highness that you made an impression upon all those who had the satisfaction to be near you at that period which will not easily be effaced, and that you have the most anxious wishes of us all for your prosperity and happiness. As to my part, I shall always look to the interesting career which you have to run with an anxiety which can be more easily felt than described, which has for its object not only your own individual happiness, but the security and happiness of the civilized world. (*To H. R. H. the Prince of Orange, G.C.B. Paris,* 14*th Nov.* 1815.)

Newspaper "Lies."

My name is frequently mentioned in your newspaper, and as it is a sort of privilege of modern Englishmen to read in the daily newspapers lies respecting those who serve them, and I have been so long accustomed to be so treated, I should not have thought it necessary to trouble you on the subject, if you had not thought proper to contradict, as from authority, in a late paper, certain reports which you had before published respecting differences between the Duc de Berri and me.

This formal contradiction of certain reports tends to give the appearance of truth to certain others which remain uncontradicted, which have still less foundation in fact than those which you have been authorized to contradict. I mean, for instance, those reports which you have more than once published respecting a supposed intercourse between a certain Madame Hamelin and me. I should be justified in calling upon you to name the person who gave you the information upon this subject; nay, I believe nobody could blame me if I were to go farther; but I feel no resentment upon the subject, nor any desire to injure you. All I beg is that you will contradict these reports; and your own desire to publish only what is true respecting an individual will, probably, induce you in future to be more cautious in selecting the channel of your intelligence respecting me, when I assure you that not only I never had any intercourse or even acquaintance with Madame Hamelin, but that I never even saw her.

Other circumstances respecting me have been published in your paper which are equally false with those

I

to which I have above referred; but I will not trouble you upon them; nor should I have written to you at all, as I am really quite indifferent respecting what is read of me in the newspapers, if you had not given an appearance of truth to some reports by the formal contradiction which you have published of others. (*To ——*
——.   Paris, 24th Nov. 1815.)

CONTESTS NATURAL IN A DIVIDED COUNTRY.

It is natural that there should be violent contests in a country in which the people are divided, not only by a difference of religion, but likewise by a difference of political opinion; and that the religion of every individual is in general the sign of the political party to which he belongs; and at a moment of peculiar political interest and of weakness in the Government on account of the mutiny of the army, that the weaker party should suffer, and that much injustice and violence should be committed by individuals of the more numerous and preponderating party. (*To Messrs. —— and ——.*
Paris, 28th Nov. 1815.)

THINGS IN PARIS.

.   .   .   Things are going on tolerably here.   I do not like the Club of the Rue St. Honoré.   It is founded on Jacobinism, and if its strength should ever be consolidated, it will become dangerous.

The tail of the opposition are very busy here; and the correspondence with —— —— and —— —— active on both sides of the water.   The two latter are most violent about Ney, and we shall have that question agitated in Parliament.   —— ——, in a letter which I have seen, accuses me in pretty plain terms of allowing that " accomplished soldier to be judicially murdered, because I could not beat him in the field."

If the letter had not been shown to me confidentially, I would have prosecuted his lordship for a libel. (*To E. Cooke, Esq. Paris,* 17*th Dec.* 1815.)

TRUE ACCOUNT OF WATERLOO IMPOSSIBLE.

The Duke of Wellington presents his compliments to Sir John Sinclair, and is much obliged to him for the account of the defence of Hougoumont. The battle of Waterloo is undoubtedly one of the most interesting events of modern times, but the Duke entertains no hopes of ever seeing an account of all its details which shall be true. The detail even of the defence of Hougoumont is not exactly true, and the Duke begs leave to suggest to Sir John Sinclair that the publication of details of this kind which are not exact cannot be attended with any utility. (*Cambrai,* 13*th April,* 1816.)

WATERLOO AGAIN.

I have received your letter of the 20th. The people of England may be entitled to a detailed and accurate account of the battle of Waterloo, and I have no objection to their having it, but I do object to their being misinformed and misled by those novels called " Relations," " Impartial Accounts," &c., &c., of that transaction containing the stories which curious travellers have picked up from peasants, private soldiers, individual officers, &c., &c., and have published to the world as the truth. Hougoumont was no more fortified than La Haye Sainte; and the latter was not lost for want of fortifications, but by one of those accidents from which human affairs are never entirely exempt.

I am really disgusted with and ashamed of all that I have seen of the battle of Waterloo. The number of writings upon it would lead the world to suppose that the

British army had never fought a battle before ; and there
is not one which contains a true representation or even
an idea of the transaction; and this is because the
writers have referred as above quoted, instead of to the
official sources and reports.

It is not true that the British army was unprepared.
The story of the Greek is equally unfounded as that of
Vandamme having 46,000 men, upon which last point
I refer to Marshal Ney's Report, which upon that point
must be the best authority. (*To Sir J. Sinclair, Bart.
Bruxelles, 28th April, 1816.*)

Mistakes corrected regarding Waterloo.

.   .   .   You desire that I should point out to you
where you could receive information on this event (the
battle of Waterloo), on the truth of which you could
rely.   In answer to this desire I can refer you only to
my despatches published in the *London Gazette.* Gen.
Alava's Report is the nearest to the truth of the other
official reports published, but even that report contains
some statements that are not exactly correct.   The
others that I have seen cannot be relied upon.   To some
of these may be attributed the source of the falsehoods
since circulated through the medium of the unofficial
communications with which the press has abounded.   Of
these a remarkable instance is to be found in the report
of a meeting between Marshal Blucher and me at La
Belle Alliance, and some have gone so far as to have
seen the chair on which I sat in that farm house.   *It
happened that the meeting took place after ten at night at
the village of Genappe;* and anybody who attempts to
describe with truth the operations of the different armies
will see that it *could not be otherwise.*   The other part is
not so material; but in truth I was not off my horse

till I returned to Waterloo between eleven and twelve at night. (*To W. Mudford, Esq. Paris, 8th June,* 1816.)

The Duties of a Godfather.

Sir,—I have received your letter of the 16th March, and am highly flattered by your desire that I should stand godfather to your son.

You are aware, however, that a godfather has certain duties to perform which it is quite impossible for me to undertake in this instance, and it is at all events expected from one in the situation in which I am placed, that he should forward the views of his godson in the world. It is much the best and shortest way to state to you the fact, that there are so many officers and soldiers who have claims upon me for services rendered to the public under my command that I cannot, with justice to them, engage myself either directly or virtually to forward the views of any others. I hope, therefore, that you will excuse my standing godfather to your son, as it is really out of my power to undertake to do anything for him at any time. (*London, April 5th,* 1819.)

Remedy for a Mob.

In the existing state of things I consider 200 or 300 good infantry with a little cavalry sufficient for any mob of any numbers. Observe this, that in detaching the troops in barns, warehouses, or temporary huts, you must take great care to provide for their having good fires in the buildings in which you place them. They will otherwise be wandering about to the public houses, &c., in the neighbourhood, and they will, moreover, become unhealthy. (*To Major-Gen. Sir T. Byng. London, 21st Oct.* 1819.)

Insurgents.

Insurgents are like conquerors; they must go forward; the moment they are stopped they are lost. (*To Lord Sidmouth. Strathfieldsaye, 11th Dec.* 1819.)

Kings of Spain.

There is no country in Europe in the affairs of which foreigners can interfere with so little advantage as in those of Spain. There is no country in which foreigners are so much disliked and even despised, and whose manners and habits are so little congenial with those of the other nations of Europe. The pride and prejudice of the Spaniards, their virtues as well as their faults, are brought into action at every moment and in every transaction, and all tend to give them an exaggerated notion of their own powers and to depreciate foreigners. (*Memorandum to Viscount Castlereagh, regarding the propriety of interfering in Spanish Affairs. London, 16th April,* 1820.)

Room to move.

Nothing can be so erroneous as to place any individual of great activity and talents in a situation in which there is no scope for his activity, and in which he must feel that his talents are thrown away. His views must always be directly to disturb rather than to preserve the existing order of things, in order that out of a new arrangement he may find himself in a position better suited to him. (*Memorandum upon appointing Mr. Canning to office.*)

Unnecessary help in a crowd.

The following letter was addressed by the Duke to a

gentleman who fancied he had piloted him through a crowd, and who afterwards, having lost his seals, wrote to the Duke for compensation :—

"The Duke of Wellington recollects perfectly having met a gentleman in the crowd at the door of Drury-lane Theatre, on the 6th instant, who, having recognized the Duke, mentioned his name, turned about, and walked before him through the crowd to the door of the house. This service, if it can be so called, was purely voluntary on the part of this gentleman. The Duke is as well able as any other man to make his way through a crowd even if there existed any disposition to impede his progress, which did not appear, and therefore the assistance of this gentleman was not necessary; and, moreover, the Duke's footman attended him.

In stating this, however, the Duke does not deny that he considered this gentleman's conduct as very polite towards him ; and he was much flattered by it, and returned his thanks for it.

It appears that this gentleman is Mr. ———, who states he lost his seals in returning through the crowd some time afterwards, after having walked through it to the door of the theatre before Lord Palmerston ; and he desires to have compensation from the Duke for this loss.

Upon this statement, and in order to avoid making this case a precedent for others of the same kind, the Duke, however flattered by Mr. ———'s politeness, must positively deny that he has any claim upon him for compensation for his loss. The Duke does not consider that Mr. ——— rendered him any service whatever, and on the ground of service he must refuse any compensation for his loss, even if it had occurred in returning from the door of the theatre after having walked to it before the Duke.

But as Mr. —— may be a gentleman in circumstances not able to bear the expense of such a loss, and as the Duke certainly considered his conduct towards him as very polite, the Duke feels no objection to assist him to replace the loss he has sustained, at the same time taking the liberty to recommend Mr. ——, in future, to omit to render these acts of unsolicited and unnecessary politeness unless he should be in a situation to bear the probable or possible consequences. (*London, Feb.* 1821.)

Southey and the Peninsular War.

. . . In respect to Mr. Southey I have heard that he was writing a History of the War in the Peninsula, but I have never received an application from him, either directly or indirectly for information on the subject. If I had received such an application I would have told him, what I have told others, that the subject was too serious to be trifled with ; for that if any real authenticated history of that war, by an author worthy of writing it were given, it ought to convey to the public the real truth, and ought to show what nations really did when they put themselves in the situation the Spanish and Portuguese nations had placed themselves in ; and that I would give information to no author who would not write upon that principle. I think, however, that the period of the war is too near, and the character and reputation of nations as well as individuals are too much involved in the discussion of these questions for me to recommend, or even encourage, any author to write such a history as some, I fear, would encourage at the present moment. This is my opinion upon the subject in general, and I should have conveyed it to Mr. Southey if he and his friends had applied to me.

. . . I should wish you not to give Mr. Southey
any original papers from me, as that would be in fact to
involve me in his work, without attaining the object I
have in view, which is, *true* history. (*To Gen. Lord
Hill. London*, *25th Oct.* 1821.)

Sir Hudson Lowe.

I hope that Government propose to do something upon
this outrage committed upon Sir Hudson Lowe. If Sir
Hudson treated De las Casas ill (which I don't believe
he did), Government ought to disapprove of his conduct.
If he did not treat him ill, if, on the contrary, Government either approved of his conduct, or took no notice
of it at the time, they ought to protect Sir Hudson ; and,
at all events, ought not to allow a blackguard to insult
him with impunity in the streets for his conduct in the
performance of his duty.

Officers in command are but too willing to seek for
popularity ; and you may rely upon it that if you don't
take some steps to mark the sense of the Government
upon this occasion, there is no thinking man in either of
the military professions who will not feel it, and you
will not easily find another who will brave the popular
cry to serve you.

At this distance, and not knowing whether De las
Casas is still in England or not, I cannot say what
ought to be done. If he be in England, I should be for
the Attorney-General prosecuting him ; or a reward
should be offered for his apprehension ; or something
done to show that Government will not allow those who
serve the public to be assaulted with impunity. (*To
Earl Bathurst. Verona, 11th Nov.* 1822.)

. . . I answered that there was one allay of which
his Imperial Majesty had more than once availed him-

self, and that he appeared to me to have left entirely out of his calculation upon this occasion. He answered, "Which is it?" I replied, "Time!" Time would remedy many of the evils complained of as resulting from the Spanish and other revolutions. Time would strengthen France, and place her in a situation to be more able to act her part in Europe; because, in fact, it was to France that we were all to look for the danger by which we were likely to be affected, in consequence of the existence of the revolutionary principle. I then observed that I believed I considered things in France in a more favourable light than his Imperial Majesty, or than any of the ministers here; but that I could not see France go to war at present and upon a revolutionary principle, without feeling that the world was in danger, and that I would prefer to trust to time for a remedy to the mischief to be apprehended from these revolutions rather than to incur such a risk. (*Memorandum on Conversation with Emperor of Russia. Verona, 27th Nov.* 1822.)

SITUATION OF THE KING.

If the situation of the King is not what it ought to be, if he has not the power to protect himself and those employed under him in the performance of their duty in the service of the public, and if the King has not reason to be satisfied that the power allotted to him by the law is sufficient, the country will never be in a state of tranquillity, be the system of government what it may.

There will be perpetual successive insurrections in one part of the country or the other, the King and his Government will be a never-ceasing object of jealousy and mistrust, and sooner or later the catastrophe will happen which all good men deprecate. But not only is internal tranquillity impossible as long as this system lasts, but it renders foreign war and invasion certain. (*Memorandum on Spain. Jan.* 1823.)

A Cabinet Minister.

To become a member of the Government is an honourable object of ambition, and I am not astonished that a person of your talents and station should be desirous of it. But I cannot but think that I should not serve your cause nor promote your object by laying before Lord Liverpool your letter to which this is an answer. I know that it has been felt by the King and by others that the Cabinet is too numerous, and that it is objectionable to admit to it any person not holding a regular Cabinet office. It is not necessary to discuss the difference between your situation and that of Lord Sidmouth; but I am certain that if Lord Sidmouth was to relinquish his seat in the Cabinet, you would experience insurmountable difficulties in being called to fill it. In regard to the other situations to which you refer, I don't believe there is the most remote chance of any of them becoming vacant; and of this I am very certain, that your desire to belong to the Cabinet being known, which it is by what passed in 1821, and again last year, it would be much more dignified in you to wait for an offer than to bring forward your claim and your wishes upon the occasion of every move in the inferior offices of the Government.

I hope you will excuse the freedom with which I have written to you upon this subject, and will attribute it to its real motive, my desire to show you the true position of the Government in respect to the points discussed by you, and my sentiments regarding the relation in which you stand towards it. (*To the Duke of Newcastle, who wished to enter the Cabinet without office in* 1823.)

Mischief of Irish Discussions.

. . . The mischief of all these discussions and questions in Ireland is that everything is an affair of party; that inferior men in questions of this description, and in the heat of party dispute, become of far greater importance than that to which their talents and situation entitle them; that they get possession of these questions, and force from those who are their superiors, as well in station as in talents and abilities, the decision upon them. The sufferers in this contest are the unfortunate people and the nation at large, and by no means those put forward in it, much less those who really conduct and decide it.

I am convinced that there is no more moderate man than yourself, and when I entreat you to set the example of moderation, to calm the zeal and irritation of those who surround you, and to endeavour to produce all the good you can in our unfortunate country, I am convinced that I am urging that to which your own inclination would lead you. But it cannot be too often repeated, and I hope you will excuse me if I have unnecessarily repeated this recommendation upon the present occasion. (*To the Rev. D. Curtis. Woodford,* 12th *Sept.* 1824.)

Mis-statement of the Duke's Health.

. . . The newspapers have, as usual, misrepresented not only my case, of which naturally enough the editors could have known nothing, but the state of my health. The truth is, that I met with an accident in the treatment of a derangement in the ear about two years ago, by which the nerves of my head were affected and injured. My stomach became consequently deranged, and although but little remains of the affection of the head, and all the unpleasant symptoms have disappeared, my health is not yet entirely re-established. I don't feel any inconvenience from the remains of this accident, excepting that I don't sleep at night quite so well as I could wish, and I must add that the act of awaking is always attended by some feeling like a quickened circulation in the head, and a corresponding feeling in the stomach. There is nothing like spasm in the case, nor ever has been ; and I really believe that time alone and attention to my diet will do me any good.

I have troubled you with this explanation in consequence of the interest which you are pleased to express about me ; but I am so tired of being the subject of the comments of the newspapers of the day, that I request you will keep this communication to yourself. (*To T. Muloch, Esq. Strathfieldsaye,* 1st *Oct.* 1824.)

Intriguing Officers.

. . . I must say that I cannot approve of officers running about to look for influence to obtain their regimental objects, instead of confiding in their own claims for employment, founded on their qualifications. I never entertain a very high opinion of these qualifications when I have such a case before me, as there is not one of them who does not know that I am well acquainted with his character and acquirements, and that if he deserves it he is quite certain of being employed as opportunities occur. (*To Sir W. Knighton. Woodford, Nov.* 26th, 1824.)

Anonymous Letter-Writing.

. . . To write, or cause to be written, an anonymous letter, is understood by gentlemen to be the dirtiest trick of which a person in that class can be guilty. (*To the Rev. Dr Curtis. Sudbourn,* 21st *Dec.* 1824.)

INVASION.

. . . I confess I am one of those who do not much apprehend invasion. I think steam navigation has in some degree altered that question to our disadvantage, particularly at the commencement of a contest, and in relation to a *coup-de-main* upon one or other of our naval arsenals. In this view of the subject, I have the officers of engineers now employed in the consideration of a plan for the security of Sheerness, which I will afterwards apply to Portsmouth and Plymouth, if I should find the Government and Parliament disposed to adopt it. But I confess that I think a solid invasion of the country, with a view even to the plunder of the capital or of Woolwich, or even to take possession of, or to do more than bombard, one of our naval arsenals, is out of the question. (*To Sir Herbert Taylor.* 27*th Dec.* 1824.)

PROSECUTION OF MR. O'CONNELL.

. . . I confess that I see more than you do. Mr. O'Connell is charged with sedition by exciting the people of Ireland to rebel, after the example of those of Colombia, and holding out hopes of their finding a Bolivar. The King says you must prosecute this man in earnest. If you hold that the people of Colombia have been guilty of no crime, and that Bolivar is a hero and no rebel, then you ought not to prosecute O'Connell. If the contrary, then you ought not to make any arrangement with that country which shall involve his Majesty in a recognition of that state beyond what is necessary.

The whole question is then open again. The reference to the example of Cromwell or Washington will not hold in this view of the case; Cromwell and Washington were equally with Bolivar rebels, and the reference to them as examples by O'Connell would have been equally seditious. But their cases are now matters of history, and the other part is wanting to the case, that we are going to bring the rebel Bolivar and the rebel state of Colombia into diplomatic relation with his Majesty, at the very moment in which we prosecute Mr. O'Connell for holding them up as examples to the people of Ireland.

This is what the King calls two half measures; and I say we cannot get out of the difficulty excepting by an explanation of what we mean very nicely worded, which in my opinion is not right. (*To the Right Hon. Robert Peel. Apethorpe*, 30th *Dec.* 1824.)

ON THE SAME SUBJECT.

You are quite mistaken if you suppose that I think O'Connell ought not to be prosecuted. I think he ought and must be prosecuted. But I confess that I agree with the King that the moment to recognize the rebel Bolivar is not luckily chosen.

I have always been of the same opinion on this subject. Bolivar is now engaged in a rebellion in Peru; and at the moment at which we are going to prosecute Mr. O'Connell for exciting the people of Ireland to rebel, we have authorized our agent in Colombia to decide whether he will or not recognize Bolivar in the name of the King; and we are in this hurry not from any cause appertaining to the case itself, but because we did not choose to take the measure which we ought to have taken—to draw from France at first the explanation which the King of France has since given in his speech to the Legislature, of the nature of the French occupation of Spain. (*To the Right Hon. Robert Peel. Apethorpe*, 2nd *Jan.* 1825.)

BEGGING FAVOURS.

When I was in India and with the army, nobody ever thought of applying for anything, knowing that I would do justice to all as fast as I could.   But these confounded corps of artillery and engineers are so accustomed to look to private patronage and applications, that I am teased out of my life by them ; and there is not a woman, or a member of Parliament, or even an acquaintance, who does not come with an application in favour of some one or other of them.   (*To Col. Malcolm.   London, Sept. 21st,* 1825.)

MEMORANDUM ON THE ROMAN CATHOLICS IN IRELAND (1825).

It must be admitted that if any arrangement can be made upon this question, the fittest time for it is one of external peace and of internal tranquillity, and when the Government is strong and universally respected.   The concessions hitherto made to the Roman Catholics have been made in times of war and of difficulty ; and it is not unreasonable to suppose that they must have produced an impression upon their minds that they were concessions to the apprehensions of the Government of their enmity and strength.   As the arrangement to be made, if made at all, must include every point which can be a subject of difference between the two religions, it is most desirable that the impression should not exist that the arrangement, whatever it may be, was extorted from our fears.

.   .   .   The evil in Ireland is of long standing, and consists entirely in the state of society.   There are two parties in that country, the *Protestants and the Roman Catholics.*   In the Protestant party are the proprietors, the clergy of the Church of England, and the mass of the Protestant population : in the Roman Catholic are the Roman Catholic bishops, clergy and gentry, and the populace, now called six millions of people.

. . . It may be stated as a general truth that there are no Protestant residents in Ireland who do not in reality apprehend the result of another contest with the Roman Catholics for the government of the country as long as the connection with England subsists, and England is in her existing state of triumphant strength, but a sudden and general rising of the populace of that religion, in which many would fall a sacrifice.

There are none who reside here who have not constantly in their minds the recollection of the histories of former rebellions ; and of those more recent of 1798 and 1803 ; and before their eyes fresh instances of the facility and secrecy with which the Roman Catholic population, even the servants in their own houses, combine for the purposes of mischief and outrage.

On the other hand, there are some Roman Catholic proprietors, and of the higher orders of the clergy, and even some of the priests, who do occasionally exert themselves to promote peace and good order. But these are exceptions to their general line of conduct. The Roman Catholic clergy, nobility, lawyers, and gentlemen having property form a sort of *theocracy* in Ireland, which in all essential points governs the populace, I believe, even to the extent of being able to *prevent* disturbance and outrage ; and by the measures of the Roman Catholic Association, and particularly the rent, this *theocracy* has acquired a knowledge of the means of organizing this mass which it had never before possessed.

This theocracy is in strict communion with the Church of Rome ; and that church continues established in

K

Ireland in all its parts, as it was three hundred years ago, with the same hierarchy, the same discipline, but ten times the authority and influence possessed by any national church whatever; although without the property belonging to the church.

. . . This, in my opinion, is the great distinction between this and other religious parties in this or any other state. The Dissenters of different descriptions in England, however troublesome and factious, and the Greeks in Hungary, are domestic parties, and have no connection with foreign powers; nor have the Greeks even in the Turkish dominions, excepting by virtue of treaties between the Porte and the Emperor of Russia. But this Roman Catholic party in Ireland is and acts in every respect as, and its existence has all the effects upon the prosperity and greatness of the empire, of a party connected with and protected by a foreign power.

Then, this formidable party not only has no connection whatever with the State, but, considering all the circumstances of preceding wars and confiscations, all upon Roman Catholic principles, and the nature of the settlement of the Government and of the property of the church and of individuals in the hands of the Protestants at the Revolution, it is obvious that it must be hostile to the Church of England, and to the connection between the two countries; and therefore to the Government. It is hostile to the Protestants, as the proprietors of the soil and the ancient instruments of the conquest, and of the suppression of the different rebellions which have taken place, and the supporters of the English connection and government. . . .

The difficulty in this most difficult question is much aggravated by the state of enmity towards the Government in which the Roman Catholics in Ireland stand, and by their determination to prevent the Crown and Church Establishment from acquiring an additional security under the Settlement. Any other sovereign, excepting his Majesty and his Majesty as King of Hanover, would upon approaching the Pope upon such a question as this have the full support of his Roman Catholic subjects in the discussion ; each class of whom would be as anxious as the King's Protestant ministers that the question should be settled in a manner honourable to the Crown, and beneficial to the public at large. But as referable to Ireland there are three parties to these questions : the King, the Pope, and the Roman Catholics in Ireland. Of these the last named are incomparably the most difficult to treat with. They will not hear of the interference of the Crown to put an end to Papal encroachment, or its consequences ; and it is obvious that their object is to prevent the exercise of any inspection or control by the Crown, in order that the country may continue under the government of the Roman Catholic theocracy. As long as the Roman Catholic religion exists in this or any other country out of the control of the Crown, it remains a system of secrecy and concealment, and therefore of danger. It has not been suffered thus to exist in any country in Europe, whether governed by a Roman Catholic or by a Protestant sovereign, and we see from antecedent transactions in Ireland, from the existing state of society in that country, and from what has come out in evidence before the committee of the Lords, that of all the countries in Europe Ireland is the one in which such a system should not be suffered to exist.

Whatever may be the opposition on the part of the Irish Roman Catholics, our view must be then to bring the Roman Catholic religion in that country under the control of the Crown; and in proportion as we shall be successful in attaining this object will the arrangement be good, and the security of the Church of England in Ireland be confirmed. Our success in this object is not less necessary for the dignity of the Crown than it is for the security of the Church, and of the Constitution and Government of the country.

It is obvious, however, that these questions cannot be so settled without an alteration of and a departure from the ancient policy of the country, from the period of the Reformation down to the present time. It must be observed that this policy was adopted in this country at the period at which the political divisions of Europe and the religious divisions were the same, and these distinctions existed till the French Revolution and its consequences annihilated church property in nearly every part of Europe. The political distinctions attending difference of religion have since become but feeble. We see the Protestant Sovereigns of Europe possessing dominions in which the Roman Catholic religion is predominant; and each of them making arrangements with the Pope of the same descriptions as the Concordats made by the Roman Catholic sovereigns, to define and regulate the spiritual authority of the Pope within their several dominions, and settling what the Roman Catholic Church shall be.

The consequence of these arrangements in every case is, that the sovereign authority becomes secure by the knowledge of and control over the actions of the Roman Catholic Church; and t. e municipal law of the country can be put in operation ir. relation to the Roman Catholic Church and its establishments, equally as upon any other establishment in the country.

SOLITARY CONFINEMENT FOR SOLDIERS.

Real solitary confinement, that is a total seclusion from all social intercourse with the whole of the human race for a given protracted space of time, the prisoner seeing nobody excepting the person charged to bring into the cell the provisions for the day, and to carry away the dirt of the cell, and during the performance of this service neither party to be allowed to utter a word, is a punishment calculated to deter men from the commission of crimes; and if such punishment is continued for any length of time, it does make an impression never to be effaced on the mind of the man on whom it is really inflicted. But it is obvious that this punishment can in reality be inflicted only in places constructed for the purpose, and under the charge of persons specially instructed as to the mode of conducting themselves with such prisoners, and who will carry into execution strictly such instructions.

These prisoners must have one or more sentries over them. Is it not certain that these sentries will talk to their prisoners in solitary confinement? If anybody can communicate with the prisoner there is an end to his solitary confinement.

. . . I have seen confinement of the nature contemplated by Colonel Woodford practised in the service at Fort William, in Bengal.

For trifling offences, not necessary to be brought under the consideration of a court-martial, such as drunkenness, &c., soldiers are there confined in what is called the *conjee-house*, by the commanding officer, for a period not exceeding forty-eight hours. They are there fed upon *conjee* alone, that is the water in which rice has been boiled; they are locked up in what are intended to be solitary cells, that is to say one man in each place of confinement.   But they are under the charge of sentries, and no man who ever knew what British soldiers are, ever believed that they did not talk to whom they pleased.

. . .   This description of punishment was in hot climates not otherwise than beneficial to the health of the men on whom it was inflicted, but I never found or heard that it had any effect upon their conduct.   (*Ordnance Office, 8th Sept.* 1825.)

Slave Traffic.   (1826.)

The traffic in slaves on the coast of Africa has doubled, while the market for their sale has diminished almost to nothing ; and it must be admitted that the measures adopted by his Majesty's Government to put an end to the traffic, however expensive in lives as well as money, have totally failed in producing any effect.

British Cavalry.   (1826.)

I considered our cavalry so inferior to that of the French, from want of order, although I consider one squadron a match for two French squadrons, that I should not have liked to see four British squadrons opposed to four French ; and as the numbers increased, and order, of course, became more necessary, I was more unwilling to risk our cavalry without having a greater superiority of numbers.

The Failure of the Potato Crop.   (1826.)

The total failure of the potato crop, if it occurs, must deprive the country labourers, who are paid by gardens or by con-acres, not only of the food on which they subsist, but of the wages of their labour. . . . This is the way, then, in which we shall stand in Ireland, if the calamity of the total failure of the potato crop should fall upon us, in addition to that of the failure of the oat crop. (1.) We must fill the markets with oats, barley, or some other food, for the consumption of that part of the population who have hitherto been fed from the markets. (2.) We must supply food for those who have hitherto been fed from their own gardens, &c. If I am not mistaken this is the whole of the country population of the three southern provinces. (3.) We must contrive the means of distributing this food.

SPEECHES IN PARLIAMENT.

 OW I have been informed that in several Roman Catholic schools children have been taught to read, not out of the Bible, but out of "Paine's Rights of Man," and in books professing to give an account of the sufferings and ill-treatment which the Roman Catholics of Ireland have experienced at the hands of the Protestants. Such an education as this, it is evident, must necessarily breed them up in a fixed and rooted hatred to Protestants. (*April*, 1828.)

ON THE CORPORATION AND TEST ACTS.

I am not one of those who consider that the best means of preserving the Constitution of this country is by rigidly adhering to measures which were called for by particular circumstances, because those measures have been in existence for two hundred years, for the lapse of time might render it proper to modify if not to remove them altogether. (*April 21st*, 1828.)

THE CHARACTER OF THE ARMY.

I confess I have great objections to allow any one who has been guilty of a crime to serve in the army as a soldier. I do not mean to say that there are not many persons in the army who have been guilty of crimes, but I do not wish to have them as having committed crimes. What I object to is this, that persons should be sent to serve in the army or navy as a punishment for committing a crime. Such a mode of enlistment is not at all calculated, in my opinion, to ensure the good conduct of the army or navy, and I shall, therefore, certainly object to the clause. (*May* 16*th*, 1828.)

Roman Catholic Disabilities.

My Lords, I have never objected to the Roman Catholics on the ground that they believe in transubstantiation, or in purgatory, or in any other of those peculiar doctrines by which they are distinguished,—doctrines with which a most reverend prelate (Canterbury) conceived it to be his duty to find fault. But I have objected to the admission to offices of trust and power of persons believing in those doctrines, because the conduct and opinions of those persons was considered, in other respects, to be inconsistent with the principles of the Constitution and the safety of the State. . . . The question, then, is one merely of expediency ; and I ground my opposition not on any doctrinal points, but on the church government of the Roman Catholic religion. . . . I must observe that nobody can have looked into the transactions in Ireland for the last hundred and fifty years without at the same time seeing that the Roman Catholic Church has acted on the principle of a combination ; that this combination has been the instrument by which all the evil that has been done has been effected ; and that to this cause the existing state of things in Ireland is to be attributed. (*June* 10*th*, 1828.)

Buckingham Palace.

. . . I must say, notwithstanding the expense which has been incurred in building the palace (Buckingham), no sovereign in Europe, I may even add, perhaps no private gentleman, is so ill lodged as the king of this country. (*July* 16*th*, 1828.)

Metropolis Police Bill.

. . . There is a point to which I wish to call your Lordships' attention, and that is the desire which so generally prevails throughout the country to diminish the number of capital punishments; and, indeed, to soften the severity of punishment in all cases. Now it seems to me, my Lords, that the best way of avoiding the infliction of punishment is to prevent the growth of crime; and we shall, I think, do much to prevent the growth of crime, and the consequent necessity of punishment, by placing an efficient police in the hands of the magistrate. (*June* 25*th*, 1829.)

Sale of Beer Bill.

As to excluding constables from keeping beer-houses, I beg to remind the noble duke that the office of constable is a burden, and that a benefit ought not to be refused to a man because a public burden has already been imposed on him. As to the clause for adding hard labour to imprisonment, I must inform the noble duke (Richmond) that the man is only to be imprisoned for nonpayment of penalties; that these penalties are a debt, and that it is not usual in legislation to inflict hard labour on a debtor. (*July* 12*th*, 1830.)

Irish Poverty.

No man either in Ireland or in England can be more painfully aware than I am of the extreme poverty of the Irish, and of the great inconvenience and danger to the empire resulting from the deplorable state of the lower orders. No person can be more sensible of all this than he who has now the honour of addressing the House; but I must beg the noble Lord to reflect that it is not by coming to this House and by talking to your Lordships of the poverty of the people that the poor can be relieved, or that the evils resulting from that poverty can be remedied. If you wish to tranquillize Ireland the way is to persuade those who have money to buy estates and settle in that country, and to employ their capital in its improvement. By transferring capital to Ireland and exciting industry there, we shall soon change the state of the case. If persons of estate and property in that country would reside in it, and spend their incomes there, they would do more to tranquillize it than all the measures which his Majesty's Ministers could adopt. (*Nov.* 2, 1830.)

The Game Laws.

. . . The killing of game forms the chief amusement of country gentlemen. It causes a large expenditure of money in the country, and affords employment to thousands of people. This expenditure of money and employment of people would cease were gentlemen deprived of the exclusive right of killing game, which they have possessed in this country for nearly five hundred years. It is worthy of observation that in every country of Europe, except France, the gentry possess the exclusive right of pursuing game. (*Sept.* 19*th*, 1831.)

Prince Talleyrand.

. . . I have no hesitation in saying that in every transaction in which I have been engaged with Prince Talleyrand, I have no hesitation, I say, in declaring that in all those transactions, from the first to the last of them, no man could have conducted himself with more firmness and ability with regard to his own country, or with more uprightness and honour in all his communications with the Ministers of other countries than Prince Talleyrand. We have heard a good deal of Prince Talleyrand from many quarters, but I feel myself bound to declare it to be my sincere and conscientious belief that no man's public and private character has been so much belied as both the public and the private character of that illustrious individual has been. I have thought it necessary, in common justice, to say this much of an individual respecting whose conduct and character I have had no slight means of forming a judgment. (*Sept. 29th*, 1831.)

Free Trade.

There is no such thing, there can be no such thing, as free trade in this country. We proceed on the system of protecting our manufactures and our produce, the produce of our labour and our soil, of protecting them for importation and protecting them for home consumption ; and on this universal system of protection it is absurd to talk of free trade. I hope this system will continue, and I shall be sorry to see the House depart from it. I concur with what the noble Lord the President of the Board of Trade has said as to the intercourse between this country and France. I am most desirous of not checking that intercourse, but that is not the question which has been brought forward by my noble friend. (*March 9th*, 1832.)

THE MAGISTRATES OF WESTMEATH.

My Lords, I regret as much as any man the warmth which creeps into the discussions on Irish subjects, and it shall always be my desire to allay it; but I beg to remind your Lordships that this irritation is not the growth of the present day: it has, in fact, existed ever since the two countries were united. . . . From my residence in Ireland I am enabled confidently to assert that no set of men are more anxious to perform the duties which they owe to the country, and to discharge the labours incident on the magisterial capacity, than the landed gentry in Ireland. They do their utmost to restore in the country the peace which it has lost, but the success of their exertions must eventually depend on their uniting with the Government. . . . I fully agree with the noble Earl (Grey) that if any force is to be called into action for the suppression of disturbances in Ireland the regular force and not the yeomanry should be employed. I do not give this opinion from any dislike of the yeomanry, on the contrary, that force appears to me most useful and constitutional; but its members are liable to be influenced, particularly in Ireland, by party spirit, which might lead them to the exercise of greater violence than might be either prudent or desirable. I should, therefore, if it be resolved to apply force, prefer voting an increase to the standing army, to the consenting to the employment of the yeomanry corps. (*April 6th*, 1832.)

A NATIONAL PASSION.

My dear Sir,—The conduct of the Ministers is a consequence of that of their predecessors in office. This is a very easy justification, but when the day of trial comes it will be found to fail altogether. Their conduct is to be attributed to neither more nor less than ancient faction, fifty years old, fears of the French, and a desire to bolster up an administration for Louis Philippe by conniving at and aiding in the national passion for domination, boasting, and bullying—that is the truth.—Believe me, ever yours most sincerely, Wellington. (*To Thomas Raikes, Esq. Strathfieldsaye, 23rd Nov. 1832.*)*

Church of England in Ireland.

Now, whatever may be thought practicable to be done with respect to the Church of England in England, I can have no objection that the same principle should be carried into effect as regards the Church of England in Ireland ; but I am afraid that the doctrine laid down in the speech from the Throne—that a different measure of reform for the Church of England may be adopted in Ireland from that which may be considered necessary to be applied to it in England—will be considered in Ireland as a breach of the Act of Union. There is yet another view of the subject which I cannot help stating, and to which I beg the particular attention of the noble Earl. It is this : that in order to maintain the Union inviolate it is absolutely necessary to pay some attention to the feelings of the Protestants of Ireland. I am happy to hear that his Majesty's Ministers are about to adopt efficient measures for restoring order in that country. . . . If any measures are to be introduced, the effect of which shall be to in-

---

* Here inserted as properly belonging to Wellington's parliamentary utterances.

duce the Protestants of Ireland to believe it is the intention of the Government to diminish the efficacy of the Church of England in Ireland, it will be impossible but that such a step must give rise to the greatest alarm; and the danger to the Church and to the empire must thereupon become indeed imminent. The Protestants of Ireland are the friends of order in Ireland, and they are the natural friends and connexions of England; and I entreat the noble Earl and your Lordships never to lose sight of this important truth. I would further beg to remind the noble Earl and the House, first, that his Majesty has sworn to maintain the Established Church of England in Ireland; and, secondly, that in the very last arrangements made to remove the disabilities as well of the Dissenters from the Church of England as of the Roman Catholics of Ireland, words were inserted in the oaths to be taken by them for the security of the Protestant Establishment. I consider these oaths as principles, and that we ought not to run counter to them in any manner whatever. (*Feb. 5th,* 1833.)

JURIES' (IRELAND) BILL.

. . . Now I would ask why is the £15 leaseholder in Ireland to be considered equal to the £20 householder in England? Is it not known that persons of the former class are men in the humbler walks of life, generally under the dominion of their priests. Are such men fit to discharge impartially the functions of jurors? Why not give the duty to those in a more elevated sphere in life, on whom we can place much greater reliance? I maintain that in Ireland it is absolutely necessary to take the administration of justice out of the hands of the lower and middle classes, and assign it to the more respectable and independent branches of the community; and further I contend that with this view, and in order to keep the administration of justice pure, the qualification of jurymen in Ireland should be higher than in this country.

. . . No country possesses greater local advantages than she (Ireland) does. Her ports, bays, and rivers give every facility for commerce ; her soil is rich, and she has a population generally disposed to industry of not less than 8,000,000 ; yet with all these advantages she is rather a burden than a relief to this country, for she does not contribute anything like one-third to the exigencies of the State, which she might do, if her resources were properly brought forth, and if a system were firmly established which would effectually secure the rights of property, and do justice between man and man. (*April* 26*th*, 1833.)

West India Slave Trade.

I tell the noble lord (Suffield) that I have done as much for the abolition of slavery and the slave trade as any man. I have been engaged in more negotiations, and have written more official notes and papers on the subject of abolition than any man now alive. There was a noble friend of mine who did still more, but with the exception of him, no man ever did more, or went further into the business, than I did, when in an official situation. (*May* 17*th*, 1833.)

Slavery.

. . . From the first occupation of the West India Colonies down to the present time the question of slavery has always been a question of difficulty and danger Over and over again it has been the cause of insurrection. It has caused more difficulties and more evils than any other question whatever. At this moment it is not more certain than it was two centuries ago that the black man can be brought to labour without that species of compulsion which is practicable only when he is in a state of slavery. It is still quite uncertain whether he can be brought to work for hire, if liberated, which after all is the real question; and therefore it is necessary to be extremely cautious in our proceedings. . . . (*June 4th*, 1833.)

GOVERNORS GENERAL.

. . . I have seen a great deal of Governors General, and have also means of judging of the nature and extent of the powers intrusted to them; and the result of my observations is a conviction that they are vested with as much power as they can desire to have, or can exercise with satisfaction to themselves or those under them. (*July 5th*, 1833.)

CHURCH TEMPORALITIES' BILL (IRELAND).

I consider the Bill entirely inconsistent with the policy of the country since the period of the Reformation, but more especially that it is inconsistent with the policy of the country since the Revolution. Since the period of the Revolution it has been the uniform object of the Parliament to maintain the Protestant Established Church in Ireland in all its integrity. That object has been clearly shown in later times—in the repeal of the Test and Corporation Acts in 1828, and in that greater measure which was introduced the year following—the measure of Catholic Emancipation. In both of those measures it was easily to be seen that the first object of Parliament was to maintain, as far as possible, the Protestant religion in Ireland as established at the Union; yet now a measure of reform in that Church is proposed to us which is contrary to all former policy, and which

L

I will maintain is the necessary consequence of the measure of last year—a measure which I cannot cease to deplore. (*July* 11*th*, 1833.)

"Agitation" in Ireland.

. . . In order that your Lordships may understand what agitation is, I will take leave to describe it. First of all it is founded upon a conspiracy of demagogues, priests, and monks, and the means are terror and mobs, to be employed wherever terror and mobs can be used. This is to produce an effect upon Ministers and an alarm in Parliament, and the mobs are excited by orations and seditious speeches at public meetings, by violent publications through the press, by exaggeration, by flattery, and by all the resources in the power of persons of that description. The people are called upon to repair in large bodies to all points where it is possible to create terror. If any person opposes himself to this design he is immediately murdered, or his house and property destroyed. The least thing is a combination to deprive him of the means of obtaining subsistence; and all is intended to destroy the peace of the country. This is the system which is called agitation. (*July* 19, 1833.)

Emancipation of the Jews.

. . . The noble and learned Lord on the woolsack has endeavoured to show that by retaining the words "upon the true faith of a Christian" upon the statute book, you encourage men who have no regard to the obligation of an oath, and thus maintain hypocrisy, while it operates as a restriction upon conscientious persons. "You admit," says the noble and learned Lord, "men like Mr. Wilkes, Lord Shaftesbury, or Lord Bolingbroke, but you shut out conscientious men who will not take the oath." I am prepared to allow that there are some men whom no oath or affirmation can reach, but this is no reason why we should give up every test and oath. Are we on this account to throw aside every guard for the maintenance of Christianity in the country? The right reverend Prelate has stated very clearly and plainly the reasons why we should not pass this Bill— namely, that this is a Christian country, and a Christian legislature, and that therefore the Parliament, composed as it is of Lords Spiritual and Temporal and Commons, cannot advise the Sovereign, as head of the Church, to sanction a law which will remove the peculiar character from the Legislature. I say that we cannot advise the Sovereign on the throne to pass a law which will admit persons to all offices, and into the Parliament of the country, who, however respectable they may be, still are not Christians, and therefore ought not to be allowed to legislate for a Christian church. The noble Marquis, for whom I entertain the highest respect, seemed surprised that I smiled when the noble Marquis spoke in somewhat extravagant terms of the distinctions which have been acquired by these persons in foreign countries. I must apologize to the noble Marquis for having smiled at that moment, but it certainly appeared to me that the noble Marquis was rather extravagant in his praise, and I may be allowed to add that I have never been so fortunate as to hear of these persons being in the stations which he described. The noble Marquis stated that there were no fewer than fifteen officers of the Jewish religion at the battle of Waterloo; I have not the least doubt that there are many officers of that religion of great merit and distinction, but still I must again repeat they are not Christians, and therefore, sitting as I do in a Christian legislature, I cannot advise the Sovereign on the throne to sanction a law to admit them to seats in this House and the other House of Parliament, and to all the rights and privileges enjoyed by Christians. (*Aug.* 1, 1833.)

ABOLITION OF SLAVERY BILL.

. . . With respect to the first topic adverted to in the Speech, as well as by the noble Duke opposite, who moved the Address, and by the noble Lord who seconded it,—I mean the Bill for the Abolition of Slavery in our West India Colonies,—I can truly say that there is no man who rejoices more sincerely than I do in the success which is stated to have attended that measure. My Lords, I certainly opposed it from its commencement ; I thought that I foresaw in that measure great injury to the interests of this country. I am very happy to find that I was deceived or misinformed in entertaining that opinion. I am afraid, however, that the noble Lords opposite are rather premature in their accounts of the entire success of that measure. I do not understand, either from what I have seen, or from what I have heard of what has passed in the West Indies, that it has entirely succeeded. . . . The state of society in the colonies we declared, by the Act we passed, should be changed from one in which slavery existed into one in which slavery should no longer be permitted to exist. The utmost the Legislature of Jamaica have done has been to adopt the law as it was passed in this country, but they have taken no measures to carry it into execution ; they have made no law to provide for the new state of society which we declared should be established ; and they have thrown the responsibility of this omission on the Government of this country. Really, my Lords, I cannot think that this is quite a successful state of affairs in the Island of Jamaica. I do not mean to charge this state of affairs upon his Majesty's Government, but I do mean to say that this is not such a state of affairs as we could have wished. (*Feb. 4, 1834.*)

Sir John Campbell.

I cannot omit the present opportunity of bearing my testimony to the respectability of Sir John Campbell, both as a British officer and as a gentleman. It appears from what the noble Earl has stated, that the Government has taken very considerable pains in order to have justice done to that gentleman. In my opinion Sir John Campbell was in the service of Don Miguel without the permission of his Majesty, and was, therefore, guilty of a breach of the Foreign Enlistment Act. But still I do not consider that he thereby forfeits his Majesty's protection when in a foreign country. (*May 6th, 1834.*)

State of Ireland.

The noble Viscount (Melbourne) has drawn a comparison between the state of this country and the state of Ireland. He has said very truly that this country would not tamely bear such provisions in Act of Parliament as are to be found even in this Bill which we are now going to pass. But, my Lords, let him show me, not only in his Majesty's dominions but anywhere, such a state of insecurity for life and property as exists in Ireland at the present moment—let him show me in any country, I care not where it is,—in the wilds of America, Africa, or Asia, such a state of society as exists at this moment in the kingdom of Ireland. I defy him to do so. (*July 29th, 1834.*)

Lord Nelson.

Some one was talking of Lord Nelson, and instances were mentioned of the egotism and vanity which derogated from his character.

" Why," said the Duke of Wellington, " I am not surprised at such instances, for Lord Nelson was in different circumstances—two quite different—even as I myself can vouch, though I only saw him once in my life, and for perhaps an hour. It was soon after I returned from India (in 1805). I went to the Colonial Office in Downing Street, and there I was shown into the waiting-room on the right hand, where I found, also waiting to see the Secretary of State, a gentleman whom, from his likeness to his pictures and the want of an arm, I immediately recognized as Lord Nelson. He could not know who I was, but he entered at once into conversation with me—if I can call it conversation—for it was almost all on his side, and all about himself, and in really a style so vain and so silly as to surprise me. I suppose something that I happened to say made him guess that I was somebody, and he went out of the room for a moment, I have no doubt to ask the office-keeper *who I was*, for when he came back he was altogether a different man, both in manner and matter. All that I had thought was a charlatan-style disappeared, and he talked of the state of this country, and of the aspect and probabilities of affairs on the Continent, with a good sense and a knowledge of subjects, both at home and abroad, that surprised me equally and more agreeably than the first part of our interview had done; in fact he talked like an officer and a statesman.

The Secretary of State kept us long waiting, and certainly, for the last half or three-quarters of an hour,

I don't know that I ever had a conversation that interested me more. Now, if the Secretary of State had been punctual, and admitted Lord Nelson in the first quarter of an hour, I should have had the same impression of a light and trivial character that other people have had; but luckily I saw enough to be satisfied that he was really a very superior man. But certainly a more sudden and complete metamorphosis I never saw. (*Walmer, Oct. 1st*, 1834.)

THE MILITIA.

The Militia is a force by which the Government is enabled at a small expense, and without keeping up an unconstitutional force, always to put the country in that state of preparation in which a great nation ought ever to be, but in which this country cannot be, in reference to the other Powers of Europe without such aid. (*Aug. 19th*, 1835.)

LOYAL SUPPORT.

. . . . I have never depended for support upon any party but the loyal subjects of his Majesty. I have never depended for support upon an individual who had been convicted of a misdemeanour, and who, after having been so convicted, was promoted by the Ministers of the Crown. (*Sept. 2nd*, 1835.)

RAILWAYS.

I certainly have a very strong feeling on the subject of all these railways to be traversed by the aid of steam. I sincerely wish that all those projects could prove successful; but in proportion as they may be successful, in the same proportion is it desirable that there should not be a perpetual monopoly established in the country. Under these circumstances I have a strong feeling that it is desirable to insert in all these Bills some clause to enable the Government or the Parliament to revise the enactments contained in them at some future specific period. I conceive that by carrying these measures into execution a very great injustice is often done to many landed proprietors in the country; and they are forced either to submit to great inconvenience, or to contend against that inconvenience by incurring a very large expense, both in this and in the other House of Parliament. If some measure of the description to which I allude be not adopted, and if these railways are to become monopolies in the hands of the present or of future proprietors, we shall hereafter be only enabled to get the better of such monopolies by forming fresh lines of road, to the further detriment of the interests of the landed proprietors, and at a great increase of expense and inconvenience. These circumstances have most forcibly struck my mind. I have had the subject under consideration for some days; I have conversed with others respecting it, and it appears to me that some plan ought to be devised in order to bring these railroads under the supervision of Parliament at some future period. (*June 3rd,* 1836.)

Post-Office Commissioners Bill.

There can, my Lords, be no doubt whatever that the Post-Office is one of the most important departments of the Government, and that his Majesty's Ministers are highly interested in the good management of that department. . . . I know enough of the working of the Post-Office to be able to say that it has worked well. It is quite certain that up to this period the Post-Office has been administered in a way highly beneficial to his Majesty's service, and I will say, that administered as it

is, it is far better administered than any Post-Office in
Europe, or any other part of the world; and before I
make any change in the administration of that office
I should like to see the grounds on which the change is
sought to be made. I do not care whether the Post-
master-General is to have a seat in this House, or
whether the head of the Post-Office shall be a Member
of the House of Commons, though that is not, in my
opinion, an unimportant part of the question, but I
want to know the grounds on which it is recommended
to make a Board of Commissioners and two or three
Secretaries for England, Ireland, and Scotland. (*Aug.*
12*th*, 1836.)

IRISH PROTESTANT PETITION.

I always had the greatest disinclination to take a part
in the discussions of such questions as the present, but
under the circumstances of the case I feel myself called
upon to offer a few observations to your Lordships. It
has, my Lords, been always my wish, my sincerest wish,
a wish which I have frequently stated to this House, to
see the Protestants of Ireland on the best possible terms
with the Government, and to see that Government
affording to them every protection in its power. It is
my firm and decided conviction that the safety of this
country, that the continuance of the Union and the
stability of the empire, are in a great measure, if not
entirely, dependent upon the good understanding existing between the Government of Ireland and the Protestant population of that country. I am also equally
certain that, safety for Protestant property and Protestant person in Ireland must mainly depend upon the
good understanding which exists between them and the
Government. Matters can never by possibility go right

without such an understanding. This, my Lords, was my opinion expressed seven years ago, and it is an opinion in which I am now even more and more confirmed. (*April* 28*th*, 1837.)

Municipal Corporations (Ireland).

. . . Now in forming corporations for Ireland the greatest possible care should be taken, first of all, that no injury should be done to the Church, that no establishment should be formed that could prove injurious to the Church, and in the next place, that by every means in our power we should take care nothing we did should give an influence, a paramount influence, to those in the lower classes of society, who are most likely to be under the dictation of those who are opposed to the Protestant religion in Ireland. (*May* 5*th*, 1837.)

William IV.

It has fallen to my lot to serve his Majesty at different periods and in different situations, and while I had the happiness of doing so, upon all those occasions I have witnessed not only all the virtues ascribed to him by the noble Viscount (Melbourne), but likewise a firmness, a discretion, a candour, a justice, a spirit of conciliation towards others, and a respect for all. Probably there never was a sovereign who, in such circumstances and encompassed by so many difficulties, more successfully met them than he did upon every occasion that he had to engage them. I was induced to serve his Majesty not only from my sense of duty, not alone from the feeling that the Sovereign of this country has the right to command my services in any situation in which I consider I can be of use, but from a feeling of gratitude to his Majesty for favours conferred on me, for personal distinctions conferred on me notwithstanding that I had been unfortunately in the situation of being under the necessity of opposing myself to his Majesty's views and intentions when he was employed in a high situation under Government, and in consequence of which he had to resign a great office which he must beyond all others have been most anxious to retain ; notwithstanding that, my Lords, his Majesty employed me in his service, and he, as a sovereign, manifested towards me a kindness, condescension and favour, which long as I live I can never forget. I considered myself then not only bound by duty and the sense I feel of gratitude to all the sovereigns of this country, but more especially towards his late Majesty, to have relieved him from every difficulty I could under any circumstances. (*June 22nd*, 1837.)

QUEEN VICTORIA'S HOUSEHOLD.

I confess that it appeared to me impossible that any set of men should take charge of her Majesty's Government, without having the usual influence or control over the establishment of the Royal household—that influence and control which their immediate predecessors in office had exercised before them. (Loud cheers from the Opposition benches.) As the Royal household was formed by their predecessors in office, the possession of that influence and that control over it appears to me to be especially necessary to let the public see that the ministers who were about to enter upon office had and possessed the entire confidence of her Majesty. I considered well the nature of the formation of the Royal household under the Civil List Act, passed on the commencement of her Majesty's reign. I considered well the difference between the household of a *Queen Consort* and the household of a *Queen Regnant*, the Queen Consort not being a political person in the same light as a Queen Regnant. I considered the construction of her Majesty's household; I considered *who filled offices in it;* I considered all the circumstances attendant upon the influence of the household, and the degree of confidence which it might be necessary for the Government to repose in the members of it. I was sensible of the serious and anxious nature of the charge which the minister in possession of that control and influence over her Majesty's household would have laid upon him. I was sensible that in everything which he did, and that in every step which he took as to the household he ought to consult, not only the honour of her Majesty's Crown, and her royal state and dignity, but also her social condition, her ease, her convenience, her comfort; in short, everything which tended to the solace and happiness of her life. I reflected on all these considerations as particularly incumbent on the ministers who should take charge of the affairs of this country. I reflected on the age, the sex, the situation, and the comparative inexperience of the Sovereign on the throne; and I must say that if I had been, or if I was to be, the first person to be consulted with regard to the exercise of the influence and control in question, I would suffer any inconvenience whatever rather than take any step as to the royal household which was not compatible with her Majesty's comforts. There was another subject which I took into consideration—I mean the possibility of making any conditions or stipulations in respect to the exercise of this influence and control over the household. It appeared to me that the person about to undertake the direction of the affairs of this country who should make such stipulations or conditions, would do neither more nor less than this,—stipulate that he would not perform his duty, that he would not advise the Crown in a case in which he thought it his duty to advise the Crown, in order that he might obtain place. I thought that no man could make such a stipulation, and consider himself worthy of her Majesty's confidence, or entitled to conduct the affairs of the country. I thought it impossible that such a stipulation should be made. Nor did I think it possible that the Sovereign could propose such a stipulation or condition to any one whom her Majesty considered worthy of her confidence. (14*th May*, 1837.)

In Answer to the Queen's Speech.

My Lords, I have great satisfaction in rising upon this occasion to give my assent to the Address moved by the illustrious Prince opposite (Duke of Sussex) in answer to the Speech delivered by her Majesty from the throne. My Lords, I have so little objection either to that gracious Speech or to the Address moved by the illustrious Prince, that I should have thought it unnecessary to address one word to your Lordships upon the subject if it had not been for the purpose of expressing my respect for her Majesty, and likewise for the illustrious Duke who has moved the Address on this occasion. I shall certainly follow the example of his Royal Highness and of the noble Lord who has seconded the Address, in making no observations, either upon the Speech or the Address which can in any manner occasion any irritation of feeling or difference of opinion on the part of any noble Lord on either side of the House. My Lords, I sincerely congratulate your Lordships that on this first occasion upon which her Majesty has addressed the Parliament called by herself, it is in the power of this House to return an answer to her Majesty which shall be unanimous! It is impossible that any noble Lords could have addressed themselves to your Lordships with more judgment and discretion than the illustrious Prince and the noble Lord who last addressed you. . . . My Lords, I hope that during every moment of the remainder of my life I shall witness the prosperity of her Majesty's reign, and her individual happiness. I can say no more, my Lords, to express my feelings towards that illustrious individual. . . . I will not trouble your Lordships further except to express an anxious hope that this Address will be allowed to pass unanimously. (*Nov.* 20, 1837.)

DISTURBANCES IN IRELAND.

. . . One of the greatest authorities that ever appeared in this or any other country—a noble relation of mine—stated that "agrarian disturbances in Ireland were to be attributed to political agitation, and to nothing else, as much as effect was to be attributed to cause in any instance whatever. (*Nov.* 27, 1837.)

PRINCIPLE OF IMPRISONMENT FOR DEBT.

One of the causes of debt being incurred in this country is, in a great degree, the power which creditors at present possess to arrest their debtors upon *mesne* process; and I still further believe that it is the facility which is thus given of obtaining credit that has been the cause of the great mercantile prosperity of the country. The enormous transactions upon credit are such, that both individuals and the public generally, require further means of recovering debts than exist in other countries. (*Dec. 5th,* 1837.)

A Little War.

My Lords, I entreat you, and I entreat the Government, not to forget that a great country like this can have no such thing as a little war. They must understand that if they enter on these operations they must do it on such a scale, and in such a manner, and with such determination as to the final object as to make it quite certain that those operations will succeed, and that at the very earliest possible period after the season opens. (*Jan. 10th,* 1838.)

Trades' Unions.

I rise to state my satisfaction that this subject has been taken into discussion in another place, and that a committee has been appointed to consider the combination laws in general. I cannot help expressing myself rejoiced that this subject has come thus early under the consideration of Parliament, because I believe that there is no grievance existing in any country which equals the extent of abuses that are carrying on in all parts of this united and hitherto called civilized kingdom, that equal the abuses and oppressions that are inflicted upon the labouring classes by this system of combination. I really believe, from the accounts I have seen, that there is scarcely an individual who is dependent on his labour for his subsistence, and that there is hardly any one who employs him, who has not reason to complain of these combinations. (*Feb. 15th,* 1838.)

The Ballot.

My Lords, that which distinguishes us from other countries is the universal publicity of our conduct, and the open avowal of our sentiments to all mankind; and I should be exceedingly sorry to find men, instead of standing forward openly, and stating their opinions in the face of day, proceeding in a sneaking course, and exercising their elective franchise under a secret mode of voting. Happily the Constitution of this country has been formed not only for the protection of a limited monarchy, and of those interests which are immediately connected with it, but also for the protection of property. Your Lordships are called on to provide for the protection of property and the security of the Church, as well as for the security of liberty and life; and I hope that in all our deliberations we shall never lose sight of those most important objects. (*Feb.* 23*rd,* 1848.)

A Free Press in Malta.

I was much struck on reading the Report which I now hold in my hand. It appears to have been sent to Malta for one purpose, and one only; it has effected one purpose and one only; it has produced a Report on a free press, and has enabled the noble Lord to write that despatch which he wrote eight months after he received the Report. The Commission was appointed in September to inquire into a variety of matters connected with the government of Malta; but it struck out nothing, and, as my noble friend says, reported on nothing for the first few months, except drawing up that proposition for the establishment of a free press. His Majesty, in the Commission he issued, called the attention of the Commissioners to a variety of subjects connected with the civil government of the Island of Malta, but that which the Commission does not mention—certainly it is not excluded—are the words "Free Press." It does not say one syllable about the press. What, however, did the Commission? They were appointed in the month of September, they landed in Malta in the month of October, and the first thing they did was to commence an inquiry into the state of the press, as if that matter was the most important and pressing of the matters that interested the island. At the end of six months they made a report, which has been received.

I beg your Lordships to recollect what Malta is. It is a fortress and a seaport, a great naval and military arsenal in the Mediterranean. We hold it by conquest and by treaty after conquest. We hold it as a great military and naval arsenal, and as nothing else. Why, we might just as well talk of putting a free press on board the admiral's ship of the line in the Mediterranean, of setting it up in the garrison of Gibraltar, or of sending it into the quarters of Sir John Colborne in North America. A free press in Malta! The very idea is contemptible. A free press in the Italian language in Malta! Malta contains 100,000 inhabitants, and the report itself tells us that the greater proportion of those inhabitants cannot understand the Italian language. They do not want a free press to watch the manner in which the English soldiers and sailors perform their duty. What can they want with a free press in Malta, when we are told that the working population there speak no language but the Maltese? It is proposed to establish a free press for a population who do not understand the language in which it is to be published, and who, if they do understand it, can neither read nor write. (*May 3rd*, 1838.)

MISCELLANEOUS ANECDOTES, LETTERS, ETC.*

HAYDON'S VISIT TO THE DUKE OF WELLINGTON.

Walmer Castle, *Oct.* 9, 1839.

HE Duke of Wellington presents his compliments to Mr. Haydon. If Mr. Haydon will be so kind as to come to Walmer Castle whenever it may suit him, the Duke will have it in his power to sit to him for a picture for certain gentlemen at Liverpool."

This invitation was eagerly accepted, and the journal which follows has this very full account of it: "October 11th, left town by steam for Ramsgate. Got in at half-past six, dined and set off in a chaise for Walmer, where I arrived safely in hard rain. A great bell was rung on my arrival; and after taking tea and dressing, I was ushered into the drawing-room where sat his Grace, with Sir Astley Cooper, Mr. Arbuthnot, and Mr.

[* It has been thought fit to add to the utterances of the great Duke certain anecdotes from various sources, as well as separate ana and maxims of the speaker. It has been found difficult to assign dates to the majority of these, and they are therefore left without any attempt at classification.—ED. *Bayard Series.*]

Booth, who had served with his Grace in Spain. His Grace welcomed me heartily, asked how I came down, and fell again into general conversation. He talked of ——, who kept the Ship. He married an actress from Astley's. She was a fine lady and the Duke said, 'I soon saw all would go wrong one day, for whilst I was there, somebody said he wanted something, and madame, with the air of a Duchess, replied, 'she would send the housemaid.' That wouldn't do. —— became bankrupt; and there were trinkets belonging to her; but she preferred her trinkets to her honour, and swore she was not his wife.' The Duke talked of the sea encroaching at Dover, and of the various plans to stop it. 'What! there are plans?' said Sir Astley. 'Yes, yes, there are as many Dover doctors as other doctors,' said he; and we all laughed.

"The Duke talked of Buonaparte and the Abbé du Pradt, and said 'there was nothing like hearing both sides.' Du Pradt in his book (he was *à fureur de memoires*) says, that whilst a certain conversation took place at Warsaw, between him and Napoleon, the Emperor was taking notes. At Elba, Napoleon told Douglas, who told the Duke, that the note he was taking was a note to Maret (Duke of Bassano) as follows: 'Renvoyez ce coquin là à son archevêque.' 'So,' said the Duke, 'always hear both sides.' The Duke said when he came through Paris, in 1814, Madame de Stael had a grand party to meet him. Du Pradt was there. In conversation he said, 'Europe owes her salvation to one man. But before he gave me time to look foolish,' added the Duke, 'Du Pradt put his hand on his own breast and said, *C'est moi!*'

"He then talked of Buonaparte's system. Sir Astley used the old cant—'It was selfish.' 'It was,' said the

Duke, 'bullying and driving.' Of France, he said, 'They robbed each other and then poured out on Europe to fill their stomachs and pockets by robbing others.'

"He spoke of Don Carlos—said he was a poor creature. He saw him at Dorchester House, two days before he escaped. He advised him not to think of it. He told him ' All we are now saying will be in Downing Street in two hours, you have no post.' Carlos said, ' Zumalacarraguy will take me on.' 'Before you move,' replied his Grace, ' be sure *he* has got one.' (Here was the *man*.) The Duke said Carlos affected sickness—somebody got into his bed and kept the farce up—that medicine came— that the French ambassador behaved like a noodle. Instead of telegraphing up to Bayonne, which would have carried the news there in two hours, he set off in his post carriage and four after Don Carlos, when he must have got to Bayonne, or near it.

"The Duke talked of the want of fuel in Spain—of what the troops suffered, and how whole houses, so many to a division, were pulled down regularly, and paid for, to serve as fuel. He said every Englishman who has a home goes to bed at night. He found bivouacking was not suitable to the character of the English soldier. He got drunk and lay down under any hedge. Discipline was destroyed. But when he introduced tents, every soldier belonged to his tent, and drunk or sober, he got to it, before he went to sleep. I said, ' Your Grace, the French always bivouac.' ' Yes,' he replied, ' because French, Spanish, and all other nations, lie anywhere. It is their habit. They have no homes.'

"The Duke said the natural state of man was plunder. Society was based on security of property alone. It was for that object men associated ; and he thought we were coming to the natural state of society very fast.

"I studied his fine head intensely. Arbuthnot had begun to doze. I was like a lamp newly trimmed, and could have listened all night. The Duke gave a tremendous yawn, and said, 'It is time to go to bed.' Candles were rung for. He took two and lighted them himself. The rest lighted their own. The Duke took one and gave me (being the stranger) the other, and led the way. At an old view of Dover in the hall, he stopped and explained about the encroachments of the sea. I studied him again—we all held up our candles. . . .

"12th. At ten we breakfasted—the Duke, Sir Astley, Mr. Booth, and myself. He put me on his right. 'Which will ye have, black tea or green?' 'Black, your Grace.' 'Bring black.' Black was brought, and I ate a hearty breakfast. In the midst, six dear healthy noisy children were brought to the windows. 'Let them in,' said the Duke, and in they came, and rushed over to him saying, 'How d'ye do, Duke? How d'ye do, Duke?' One boy, young Grey, roared, 'I want some tea, Duke.' 'You shall have it, if you promise not to slop it over me as you did yesterday.' Toast and tea were then in demand. Three got on one side and three on the other, and he hugged 'em all. Tea was poured out, and I saw little Grey try to slop it over the Duke's frock coat. Sir Astley said, 'You did not expect to see this.' They all then rushed out on the leads by the cannon, and after breakfast I saw the Duke romping with the whole of them, and one of them gave his Grace a devil of a thump. . . . .

"He told me to choose my room and get my light in order, and after hunting he would sit. I did so, and about two he gave me an hour and a half. I hit his grand, upright, manly expression. He looked like an eagle of the gods who had put on human shape, and had got silvery with age and service. At first I was a little affected, but I hit his features, and all went off. Riding had made him rosy and dozy. His colour was fresh. All the portraits are too pale. I found that to imagine he could not go through any duty raised the lion. 'Does the light hurt your Grace's eyes?' 'Not at all;' and he stared at the light as much as to say, 'I'll see if you shall make me give in, Signor Light.'

"'Twas a noble head. I saw nothing of that peculiar expression of mouth the sculptors give him, bordering on simpering. His colour was beautiful and fleshy, his lips compressed and energetic. I foolishly said, 'Don't let me fatigue your Grace.' 'Well sir,' he said, 'I'll give you an hour and a half. To-morrow is Sunday, Monday I'll sit again.'   .   .   .

"At seven we dined. His Grace took half a glass of sherry and put it in water. I drank three glasses, Mr. Arbuthnot one. We then went to the drawing-room, where, putting a candle on each side of him, he read the Standard whilst I talked to Mr. Arbuthnot, who said it was not true Copenhagen ran away on the field. He ran to his stable when the Duke came to Waterloo, after the battle, and kicked out and gambolled.

"I did not stay up to-night. I was tired, went to bed, and slept heartily. It was most interesting to see him reading away. I believe he read every iota. We talked of Lord Mulgrave whom his Grace esteemed. Sir Astley had left in the morning, and in talking of the Duke's power of conversation, related that when some one said, 'Habit is second nature,' the Duke remarked, 'It is ten times nature.'

"I asked the Duke if Cæsar did not land hereabouts. He said he believed near Richborough Castle.

"Sunday, I found the Duke on the leads. After breakfast Mr. Arbuthnot told me to go to the village church and ask for the Duke's pew. I walked there, and was shown into a large pew near the pulpit.

"A few moments after the service had begun, the Duke and Mr. Arbuthnot came up—no pomp, no servants in livery with a pile of books. The Duke came into the presence of his Maker without cant, without affectation—a simple human being.

"From the bare wainscot, the absence of curtains, the dirty green footstools, and common chairs, I feared I was in the wrong pew, and very quietly sat myself down in the Duke's place. Mr. Arbuthnot squeezed my arm before it was too late, and I crossed in an instant. The Duke pulled out his prayer-book, and followed the clergyman in the simplest way. I got deeply affected. . . . At the name of Jesus Christ the Duke bowed his silvery hairs like the humblest labourer, and yet not more than others, but to the same degree. He seemed to wish for no distinction. At the epistle he stood upright like a soldier, and when the blessing was pronounced he buried his head in one hand, and uttered his prayer as if it came from his heart in humbleness. . . .

"The Duke after dinner retired, and we all followed him. He then took the 'Spectator,' and placing a candle on each side of his venerable head, read it through. I watched him the whole time. Young Lucas had arrived—a very nice fellow—and we both watched him.

". . . After reading till his eyes were tired, he put down the paper and said, 'There are a great many curious things in it, I assure you.' He then yawned, as he always did before retiring, and said, 'I'll give you an early sitting to-morrow at nine.' . . . By nine the door opened and in he walked, looking extremely worn—his skin drawn tight over his face; his

eye was watery and aged, his head nodded a little. I
put the chair, he mumbled, 'I'd as soon stand.' I
thought he would get tired, but I said nothing. Down
he sat—how altered from the fresh old man after Satur-
day's hunting! It affected me. He looked like an eagle
beginning to totter from his perch. He took out his
watch three times, and at ten up he got and said, ' It's
ten.' I opened the door and he went out. He had
been impatient all the time. At breakfast he bright-
ened at the sight of the children, and, after distributing
toast and tea to them, I got him on art. He talked of
a picture of Copenhagen by Ward, which the Duke of
Northumberland bought, and which he wanted, and
suddenly looking up at me said, 'D'ye want another
sitting?' 'If you please, your Grace.' 'Very well,
after hunting I'll come.' Just as he was going hunting, or whilst he was out, came Count Brunow, the
locum tenens of Pozzo di Borgo, the Russian Ambassador. Lady Burghersh came in from Lady Marlbo-
rough's, and Mr. Arbuthnot wanted her to go in and
talk to Brunow, but she declined. All of a sudden I
heard a great clatter, and the servants came in to move
the great table for lunch. At lunch I was called
in. The Duke, Count Brunow, and myself lunched.
At three he came in, having sent Brunow with
Arbuthnot *pour faire un tour.* Lady Burghersh came
in also; and again he was fresher, but the feebleness of
the morning still affected my heart. It is evident at
times he is beginning to sink, though the sea air at
Walmer keeps him up, and he is better than he was.

Lady Burghersh kept him talking, but the expression
I had already hit was much finer than the present, and
I resolved not to endanger what I had secured. I
therefore corrected the figure and shoulders, and told

Lady Burghersh I had done. 'He has done' said she, 'and it's very fine.' 'Is it though?' said the Duke; 'I'm very glad.' 'And now,' said she, 'you must stand.' So up he got, and I sketched two views of his back, his hands, legs, &c. &c. I did him so instantaneously that his eagle eyes looked me right through several times, when he thought I was not looking. As it was a point of honour with him not to see any sketch connected with my picture he never glanced that way. He looked at the designs for the House of Lords on the chimney-piece, but said nothing. He then retired, and appeared gay and better. He had put on a fine dashing waistcoat for the Russian Ambassador.

"At lunch the Duke said, in the churches of Russia he never heard a single cough in the coldest weather.

"At dinner there was a party—Lord and Lady Mahon; Colonel D——, a captain of Horse Artillery; Brunow; Captain V——, and several others. Colonel D—— had the Waterloo medal and legion of honour. He was a spirited fellow, but had too much of the mess-table, which is all affected sentiment, boasting justice to the enemies of England, and, in fact, unideal chatter over claret and champagne. Captain V—— was an honest old boy.

"The Duke looked well, and told some stories. As Lady Stuart was coming from the tournament with a friend they got into a railway carriage, where sat a man who did not move, so they sat down beside him. At last in came another, who begged one of the ladies to sit up, because he must sit by 'his convict.'

"At night, as I took leave of the Duke, he said, 'I hope you are satisfied. Good-bye.' I heard him go to bed after me, laughing, and he roared out to Arbuthnot, 'Good night.' I then heard him slam the door of his room, No. 11, next to mine, No. 10, but on the opposite side, and a little further on. I soon fell asleep ; was off at six for Ramsgate, and dined at home at five."*

INVASION AT BOULOGNE.

Since I wrote to you last a *terrible event* has taken place. I mean the expedition of Louis Napoleon to Boulogne. Those desirous of fomenting the existing differences and jealousies between the countries will avail themselves of this event to promote their objects. (*To T. Raikes, Esq. Aug. 8th*, 1840.)

THE PRESS.

It appears to me that the newspapers here and in France are again becoming less pacific. I conclude that they write what will please their readers ; and upon such a question as that which now occupies the minds of men, they write in the sense most agreeable to their friends among the public. I sincerely wish that I could see a chance of bringing this affair to a termination calculated to secure the peace of the world. (*To T. Raikes, Esq. Walmer Castle, Sept. 5th*, 1840.)

PEACE WITH FRANCE.

I cannot but feel hope that we may yet see peace preserved between these two nations, whose interest is, on both sides, so essentially involved in its preservation. I think I see daylight. But it is difficult to form a judgment of any event in which such multitudes take an active part, and are so little reasonable. A little sound sense on both sides would have a wonderful effect. (*Ibid. Sept.* 12th, 1840.)

---

* From Tom Taylor's " Life of Haydon."

ATTITUDE OF ENGLAND.

I am certain that there is no desire in this country on the part of any party, I may almost say of any influential individual, to quarrel with, much less to do anything offensive, towards France. But if we should be under the necessity of going to war, you will witness the most extraordinary exertions ever made by this or any country in order to carry the same on with vigour, however undesirable we may think it to enter into it. (*To T. Raikes, Esq. Walmer Castle, Oct. 4th, 1840.*)

ESCAPE OF LOUIS PHILIPPE.

. . . It is very clear to me that Louis Philippe has had a narrow escape. He would probably have been involved in naval or military difficulties, and then his state would have been the same as that of all sovereigns involved in foreign war by domestic factions, who cannot or will not supply the means of carrying on the operations of the same so as to be successful, and then those who occasion the war are loudest in their complaints of disgrace, and the public are to be satisfied by hurling the sovereign from the throne, and a fresh revolution. This is the natural and usual course of such events and transactions. (*To T. Raikes, Esq. Walmer Castle, Nov. 4th, 1840.*)

RISK OF WAR.

. . . Of this I am very certain,—any power who should commence a war upon another must well consider its necessity, and the risks and dangers to be incurred by commencing it on the one hand, and by avoiding it on the other. (*To T. Raikes, Esq. Walmer Castle, Nov. 9th, 1840.*)

France and England.

. . . My opinion is that France and England at peace, respecting each other, and each the rights of the other, are strong enough to preserve the general peace, and to prevent the oppression of the weak of this world by the strong. (*To T. Raikes, Esq. Strathfieldsaye, Dec.* 23rd, 1840.)

Isolation.

. . . I have no confidence in the system of *isolement* (isolation). It does not answer in social life for individuals, nor in politics for nations. Man is a social animal. (*To T. Raikes, Esq. London, March* 1st, 1841.)

Hatred of England.

The detestation of *us* in France is *wonderful*. But not more so than the total apathy and indifference with which is viewed in England this state of the feelings of men in France. (*To T. Raikes, Esq. Walmer Castle, Aug.* 30th, 1842.)

Difficulties.

I am certain that it is possible for a government, as well as for individuals in the world, to avoid being involved in difficulties. (*To T. Raikes, Esq. Strathfieldsaye, Dec.* 1st, 1842.)

Political Study.

In these times of political and democratical intrigue, it is impossible to acquire at first sight the truth upon any subject. It can be acquired only by laborious study. . . . . Men are under the necessity of judging of what passes before their eyes, by referring to antecedent circumstances, and to the known course of the same parties on former and similar occasions. (*To T. Raikes, Esq. Strathfieldsaye, Jan. 4th,* 1843)

DEATH-BED CONVERSIONS.

I am sorry for poor Moutrond, but pleased that he died a Christian. I don't believe that these sudden death-bed conversions are of good example; but it is better that such should take place for such a man as he was rather than not at all. They produce some effect on those who imitate them, and the few who admire them. I don't think that his last moments were calculated to conciliate the generality of the society at Paris, or in France, who rarely think seriously upon any subject. (*To T. Raikes, Esq. Walmer Castle, Oct.* 23*rd,* 1843.)

CHARITY TO ALL.

We must make the most of men as we find them; and of the circumstances of the times in which we live, and do our best, each in his position, to protect our country and the world from the evils by which we are threatened. (*To T. Raikes, Esq. London, Nov.* 18*th,* 1843.)

WONDERFUL TIMES.

We are living in wonderful times. The spirit of democracy has taken a start, and made a progress everywhere which astounds us; as if the last occasion of what we witness were a first instance, notwithstanding that they are of daily occurrence everywhere. (*To T. Raikes, Esq. Strathfieldsaye, May* 27*th,* 1844.)

WE have absolutely no detailed record of the sayings and doings of Arthur Wellesley Duke of Wellington when a boy. He rarely spoke of those days himself, and never with pleasure. He went when quite young to a preparatory school at Chelsea, where his father, Lord Wellesley, called to see him, and gave him a shilling. From Chelsea he was removed to Eton, where history is almost silent upon the subject of his sayings and doings. Upon the death of Lord Mornington, after a while Lord Wellesley took his son Arthur to Brussels, where he was instructed by the Avocat Goubert, whose house he recognized after Waterloo.

ARTHUR WESLEY AT ETON.

Robert, or as he was usually called, Bobus Smith, brother to the celebrated Reverend Sidney Smith, was one day bathing in the Thames when Arthur Wesley, not then Wellesley, passed by. For fun Arthur threw a clod at the bather, and Bobus cried out, " If you do that again I will get out and thrash you." As a matter of course another and yet another clod were thrown, and Bobus landed, and without waiting to dress, struck the first blow. A sharp battle ensued, which ended in favour of the youth who certainly had not moral right on his side. This, however simple and common-place, " is all that history or tradition tells us," says the Rev. G. R. Gleig, " of the Eton days of the greatest man whom Eton itself has ever produced."

The Duke with his Sons.

It is said that when Wellington took down his sons to enter them at Eton, he pointed out a particular tree, upon which one day having climbed he sat, and " seated there sketched out to himself the whole of his future career." (*Rev. G. R. Gleig*, who thinks that the story is improbable.)

Lady Dungannon Hoaxed.

Arthur Wesley, and his brothers at Eton with him, were once invited to spend their holidays with Lady Dungannon in Shropshire, and, full of fun, they determined to tell her ladyship some startling piece of news, of course utterly without foundation. They informed her that their sister Anne had run off with the footman, begging her not to mention the circumstance on any account. Her gossipping ladyship suddenly remembered a visit she owed to Mrs. Mytton, a neighbour of hers, to whom she communicated the intelligence. Returning, she said, to the boys, to their overwhelming amusement, " Ah, my dear boys, ill news travels apace. Will you believe it? Mrs. Mytton knew all about poor Anne."

Lieutenant Wesley.

On 21st March, 1787, Mr. Wesley was made an ensign; on the 25th December, a lieutenant of the 41st Foot. He was still a shy awkward lad in whom the ladies saw nothing to admire. At a ball one night as Lady Alborough tells the story, he could find no partner, and inheriting his father's taste for music, he consoled himself by sitting down near the band. When the party broke up, and the other officers were taken home by their lady friends, young Wesley was left by common consent to travel with the fiddlers. When he had become a great man Lady Alborough reminded him of the circumstance, adding with *naïveté*, "We should not leave you to go home with the fiddlers now."

A Soldier's Weight.

Shortly after Wesley joined his first regiment as ensign, he caused a private soldier to be *weighed*, first in full marching order, arms, accoutrements, ammunition, &c., and afterwards without them. "I wished," he said, "to have some measure of the power of the individual man compared with the weight he was to carry, and the work he was expected to do. I was not so young as not to know that since I had undertaken a profession I had better endeavour to understand it. It must always be kept in mind that the power of the greatest armies depends upon what the individual soldier is capable of doing and bearing."

Supposing.

In the Peninsula, when an officer of rank joined the Duke, he was asked to dine at head-quarters on the Duke's right hand. Military questions were not generally discussed, but on one occasion, a major-general so perseveringly questioned the Duke as to his critical position at the time that the Field-Marshal condescended to ask him his opinion. "Supposing," said the Major-General, "the French moved here, and there, and then there (making marks upon the table-cloth), which they inevitably *would* do, then what would your Grace do?" "Give them the most infernal thrashing they have had for some time," was the reply. The interlocutor, it is needless to add, was effectually silenced.

A BAD EGG.

Dining on the morning of one of his battles with Lord Fitzroy Somerset, the Duke made dreadfully wry faces while eating his egg, at the same time appearing to be absorbed in thought. At last, apparently recollecting himself, he said, " By the bye, Fitzroy, is that egg of yours fresh? for mine was quite rotten."

HOOKY-NOSE.

During the siege of Burgos, one of the Irish regiments displeased Wellington greatly by not acting with necessary bravery; to make up for their supposed neglect, they begged permission to lead the assault next time. They were allowed their wish, and nearly all destroyed. Sir Arthur rode up to a heap of slain and wounded. Amongst the latter was a man who had had both legs shot off, who saluted his commander with " Arrah, maybe ye'r satisfied now, you hooky-nosed vagabond!" The general smiled, sent a surgeon, and the audacious Hibernian lived to become an inhabitant of Chelsea Hospital.

NEVER GIVE UP.

Finding a difficulty in laying down a bridge across the Garonne, and being informed that "until the river fell a passage could not be effected," Lord Wellington instantly observed, "If it will not do one way, we must try another; for I never in my life gave up anything that I once undertook."

THE DUKE'S COOLNESS.

While the Duke of Wellington was standing in the centre of the high road in front of St. Jean, several guns were levelled against him, distinguished as he was

N

by his suite and the brilliant staff who conveyed his despatches to and fro. The bullets repeatedly grazed a tree
near him, when he observed to one of his staff, "That's
good practice; I think they fire better than in Spain."
Riding up to the 95th regiment when in front of the
line, and expecting a formidable charge of cavalry, he
said, "Stand fast, 95th; we must not be beaten. What
will they say in England?" On another occasion,
when the result of the battle seemed to be very doubtful, and some of his best and bravest men had fallen,
he said coolly, "Never mind; we'll win this battle yet."
To a regiment in a close engagement, he used a sporting ·
phrase: "Hard pounding, this, gentlemen; let's see
who will pound the longest."—*Anecdotes of Waterloo*
(1850).

After Waterloo.

On the morning of the 19th of June, Dr. Hume
entered the Duke's chamber to make his report of the
killed and wounded. He found the Duke asleep, un-
shaved and unwashed, as he had lain down late over
night. The duty being urgent, Hume awoke his chief,
and the Duke sitting up in his bed, desired him without
asking any questions to read. It was a long list, and
took a good while to go through; but after he had read
for about an hour the doctor looked up. He saw
Wellington with hands convulsively clasped together,
and the tears making long furrows on his battle-soiled
cheeks. At first the Duke did not notice that Hume
had ceased to speak, but in about a minute he cried,
"Go on," and till the reading was closed, he never once
moved from his attitude of profound grief.

The Iron Duke.

Great misapprehension prevails, both at home and abroad, concerning the origin of this *sobriquet*. The fact is it arose out of the building of an iron steamboat which plied between Liverpool and Dublin, and which its owners called the " Duke of Wellington." The term Iron Duke was first applied to the vessel ; and by-and-by, rather in jest than in earnest, it was transferred to the Duke himself. It had no reference whatever, certainly at the outset, to any peculiarities or assumed peculiarities in the Duke's disposition.

A Laconic Reply.

During the Peel Administration, an important situation in Ireland became vacant, to which an Irish relative of the Duke's wished to be appointed. He therefore wrote to his Grace, and after having stated his wish, concluded his letter with these words : " One word from your Grace will be sufficient." The Duke's reply was laconic and characteristic : " Dear ——, Not one word. —From yours affectionately, Wellington."— *The Life of Wellington* (1850).

A Life Saved.

While the allied troops were in Paris, a French citizen, passing through the Champs Elysées, where the troops were encamped, was robbed of his watch by a British sergeant. A court-martial was held upon the criminal, who was sentenced to die on the following morning. All the soldiers acknowledged the justice of the decree ; the drums beat at the appointed time, the black flag waved mournfully in the air, the ministers of justice had already raised the engines of destruction, and the fatal

word "Fire!" was almost half ejaculated, when the
Duke rushed before the firelocks, and commanded a
momentary pause, whilst he addressed the prisoner:
"You have offended against the laws of God, of honour,
and of virtue. The grave is open before you. In a few
short moments your soul will appear before its Maker.
Your prosecutor complains of the sentence—the man
whom you have robbed would plead for your life, and
is horrorstruck with the rapidity of your judgment.
You are a soldier; you have been brave, and, as report
says, until now, even virtuous. Speak boldly; in the
face of heaven, and as the soldier of an army devoted to
virtue and good order, declare now your feelings as to
your sentence." "General," said the man, "retire, and
let my comrades do their duty. When a soldier forgets
his honour life becomes disgraceful; and immediate
punishment is due as an example to the army. Fire!"
"You have spoken nobly," said the Duke, with a tear in
his eye. "You have saved your life. How can I destroy a repentant sinner, whose words are of greater
value to the army than his death would be? Soldiers,
bear this in mind, and may a sense of honour always
deter you from infamy." The troops filled the air
with their shouts. The criminal fell at the Duke's feet.
The word "March!" was given; he arose, and returned
alive in those ranks which were to have witnessed his
execution.—*The Life of Wellington* (1850).

WELLINGTON AND NELSON.

"I had an engagement with Lord Bathurst," the
Duke would say, "and found in his waiting-room a
gentleman who had lost an eye and an arm. We entered into conversation, neither of us being at all aware
of who the other might be, and I was struck with the

clearness and decision of his language, and guessed from the topics which he selected that he must be a seaman. He was called in first and had his interview; I followed, and after settling our business, Lord Bathurst asked me if I knew who had preceded me. I said 'No,' but I was pretty sure that he was no common man. 'You are quite right,' was Lord Bathurst's answer, 'and let me add that he expressed exactly the same opinions of you. That was Lord Nelson.'" He was then making his preparations for going on board the "Victory," and counted on fighting the battle in which he died.

MR. PITT.

"I did not think," said the Duke, "that Pitt would have died so soon. He died in January, 1806, and I met him at Lord Camden's in Kent, and I think that he did not seem ill, in the November previous. He was very lively, and in good spirits. It is true he was by way of being an invalid at that time. A great deal was always said about his taking his rides, for he used then to ride eighteen or twenty miles a day, and great pains were taken to send forward his luncheon, bottled porter, I think, and getting him a beef-steak or mutton-chop ready at some place fixed beforehand. That place was always mentioned to the party; so that those kept at home in the morning might join the ride there if they pleased. On coming home from those rides they used to put on dry clothes and to hold a cabinet, for all the party were members of the Cabinet, except me and, I think, the Duke of Montrose. At dinner, Mr. Pitt drank little wine; but it was at that time the fashion to sup, and he then took a great deal of port and water.

"In the same month I also met Mr. Pitt at the Lord

Mayor's dinner; he did not seem ill. On that occasion I remember he returned thanks in one of the best and neatest speeches I ever heard in my life. It was in a very few words. The Lord Mayor had proposed his health as one who had been the saviour of England, and would be the saviour of the rest of Europe. Mr. Pitt then got up, disclaimed the compliment as applied to himself, and added, 'England has saved herself by her exertions, and the rest of Europe will be saved by her example;' that was all; he was scarcely up two minutes, yet nothing could be more perfect.

"I remember another curious thing at that dinner. Erskine was there. Now Mr. Pitt had always over Erskine a great ascendancy, the ascendancy of terror. Sometimes in the House of Commons, he could keep Erskine in check by merely putting out his hand, or making a note. At this dinner Erskine's health having been drunk, and Erskine rising to return thanks, Pitt held up his finger and said to him across the table, 'Erskine, remember that they are drinking your health as a distinguished colonel of volunteers.' Erskine, who had intended, as we heard, to go off upon rights of juries, the state trials, and other political points, was quite put out; he was awed like a school-boy at school, and in his speech kept strictly within the limits enjoined him.

BLUCHER.

"I should not," said Wellington, "do justice to my own feelings, or to Marshal Blucher and the Prussian army, if I did not attribute the successful result of this arduous day to the cordial and timely assistance I received from them. The operation of General Bulow upon the enemy's flank was a most decisive one; and even if I had not found myself in a situation to make the attack which produced the final result, it would have forced the enemy to retire if his attacks should have failed, and would have prevented him from taking advantage of them if they should unfortunately have succeeded."

VIMIERO.

The lame conclusion to the battle of Vimiero might have been avoided if Sir Arthur Wellesley's advice had been taken; but Sir Harry Burrard would not be interfered with; and Sir Arthur, whose sense of military obedience would not allow him to interfere and act upon his own inferior judgment, turned to one of his officers and said, "Well, then, we have nothing to do but to go and shoot red-legged partridges."

LOUIS GOUBERT.

John Armitage, who had lived with Lady Mornington at Brussels, and been educated with her son Arthur, by Louis Goubert, met the Duke in 1827 on the grand-stand at a race, when the Duke told him this anecdote, "As I rode into Brussels the day after the battle of Waterloo, I passed the house of Louis Goubert and recognised it, and pulling up, ascertained that the old man was still alive. I sent for him, and recalling myself to his recollection, shook hands with him, and assured him that, for old acquaintance' sake, he should be protected from all molestation."

FOREIGN ENLISTMENT ACT.

" The strongest suspicion," said Wellington, " that a vessel building in the ports of this country, or about to proceed to sea, is destined to be armed elsewhere, and to become a vessel of war in the service of a belligerent; the strongest suspicion that a particular cargo of arms sailing from the ports of this country is destined for the purpose of arming that very vessel in a foreign port, would not justify the Government either in detaining the vessel or in seizing the arms, the vessel herself sailing unarmed, and the cargo of arms being entered at the Custom House as merchandise. The law applies only to what can be *proved*."

The Halt at Wilna.

" Napoleon must be supposed to have made up his mind as to what his object was in the war, and that this object was Moscow. He might then with safety have left his wings to pursue the enemy opposed to them respectively ; and he might himself, with the Guards and the 4th Corps, have moved direct upon Vitepsk from Wilna, or upon Rudnia or even upon Smolensk. He ought to have made this movement as soon as possible after his arrival at Wilna. . . . . He would have found himself at Vitepsk on the 20th of July, leaving Wilna as late as the 4th of July, with above 120,000 men between the two armies of the enemy, with no force in his front, with all their lines of communication at his mercy, and with a superior army following each of theirs."

The Greek Insurrection.

" The Greek insurrection would certainly have occurred at some time or other ; but its occurrence was accelerated for the purpose of giving matter of dispute to the two Imperial Courts, and of thus breaking up what is called the Holy Alliance. The insurrection was accelerated by those who also occasioned the Neapolitan and particularly the Piedmontese revolutions. . . . My firm belief is that the Emperor wishes for peace. .... I cannot understand the meaning of the benefit which we are to derive from the establishment in the Mediterranean of an efficient naval power which is likewise Continental. Is there, or can there be, any naval power that is not jealous of and inimical to us? Can naval affairs in the Mediterranean be better for us than they are? .... It is certainly true that the Emperor will not interfere by force in favour of the Greeks."

DEBT.

The Duke of Wellington kept an accurate detailed account of all the moneys received and expended by him. "I make a point," said he to Mr. Gleig, "of paying my own bills, and I advise every one to do the same; formerly I used to trust a confidential servant to pay them, but I was cured of that folly by receiving one morning, to my great surprise, duns of a year or two's standing. The fellow had speculated with my money, and left my bills unpaid." Talking of debt, his remark was, "It makes a slave of a man. I have often known what it was to be in want of money, but I never got into debt." (*From Self-Help*, by Mr. Smiles.)

ROUTINE.

The Duke of Wellington was a great routinist, because he was a first-rate man of business. He possessed in perfection all the qualities which constitute one. He was a most punctual man; he never received a letter without acknowledging or replying to it; and he habitually attended to the minutest details of all matters entrusted to him, whether civil or military. His business faculty was his genius, the genius of common-sense; and it is not perhaps saying too much to aver, that it was because he was a first-rate man of business that he never lost a battle. . . .

"The regiment of Colonel Wellesley," General Harris wrote in 1799, "is a model regiment; on the score of soldierly bearing, discipline, instruction and orderly behaviour, it is beyond all praise." (*From Self-Help*, by Mr. Smiles.)

DEVELOPMENT.

"The Duke's talents," says a writer in the "Edinburgh Review" of July 1859, "seem never to have developed themselves until some active and practical field for their display was placed immediately before him. He was long described by his Spartan mother, who thought him a dunce, as only 'food for powder.' He gained no sort of distinction either at Eton or at the French Military College of Angers."

A TESTIMONIAL DECLINED.

The Marquis Wellesley, on one occasion, positively refused a present of £100,000 proposed to be given him by the Directors of the East India Company on the conquest of Mysore. "It is not necessary," said he, "for me to allude to the independence of my character, and the proper dignity attaching to my office, other reasons besides these important considerations lead me to decline this testimony which is not suitable to me. *I think of nothing but our army.* I should be much distressed to curtail the share of those brave soldiers." (*From Self-Help*, by Mr. Smiles.)

EULOGY OF PEEL.

"Your Lordships," said the Duke of Wellington in the House of Lords a few days after Sir Robert Peel's death, "must all feel the high and honourable character of the late Sir Robert Peel. I was long connected with him in public life. We were both in the counsels of our Sovereign together, and I had long the honour to enjoy his private friendship. In all the course of my acquaintance with him I never knew a man in whose truth and justice I had greater confidence, or in whom I saw a more invariable desire to promote the public service. In the whole course of my communication with him I never knew an instance in which he did not show the strongest attachment to truth; and I never saw in the whole course of my life the smallest reason for suspecting that he stated anything which he did not firmly believe to be the fact."

The Word of Honour.

"When English officers," the Duke of Wellington wrote to Kellerman, when that general was opposed to him in the Peninsula, "have given their parole of honour not to escape, be sure they will not break it. Believe me, trust to their word; the word of an English officer is a surer guarantee than the vigilance of sentinels."

The Battle of Waterloo.

According to Alison, the battle of Waterloo was fought by 80,000 French, and 250 guns, against 67,000 English, Hanoverians, Belgians, &c., with 156 guns, to which were subsequently added certain large bodies of Prussians, who came in time to assist in gaining the day. There were strictly but 22,000 British troops on the field, of whom the total number killed was 1417, and wounded 4923. The total loss of the allied forces on that bloody day was 22,378, of whom there were killed 4172. When William IV. was lying on his deathbed at

Windsor, the firing for the anniversary of Waterloo took place, and on his inquiring and learning the cause, he breathed out faintly, " It was a great day for England."

WELLINGTON AND THE WORD "GLORY."

"Our own Wellington," says a recent writer, "was a far greater man than Napoleon. Not less resolute, firm, and persistent, but much more self-denying, conscientious, and truly patriotic. Napoleon's aim was 'glory;' Wellington's watchword, like Nelson's, was 'duty.' The former word, it is said, does not once occur in his despatches;* the latter often, but never accompanied by any high-sounding professions. The greatest difficulties could neither embarrass nor intimidate Wellington; his energy invariably rising in proportion to the obstacles to be surmounted. The patience, the firmness, the resolution with which he bore through the maddening vexations and gigantic difficulties of the Peninsula campaigns, is perhaps one of the sublimest things to be found in history. In Spain, Wellington not only exhibited the genius of the general, but the comprehensive wisdom of the statesman. Though his natural temper was irritable in the extreme, his high sense of duty enabled him to restrain it, and to those about him, his patience seemed absolutely inexhaustible. His great character stands untarnished by ambition, by avarice, or any low passion. Though a man of powerful individuality, he yet displayed a great variety of endowment. The equal of Napoleon in generalship, he was as prompt,

---

* This is a mistake: we give one example of his using the word in a despatch to Col. Malcolm (3rd December, 1809), showing that he by no means despised, but looked upon it, at least in the one instance under consideration, as "a solid and substantial benefit."

vigorous and daring as Clive ; as wise a statesman as Cromwell; and as pure and high-minded as Washington. The great Wellington left behind him an enduring reputation, founded on toilsome campaigns won by skilful combination, by fortitude which nothing could exhaust, by sublime daring, and perhaps still sublimer patience."

CHECKED AT BURGOS.

I once asked him whether in the case of Burgos, the government at home had been to blame for that insufficiency. "Not in the least," was the reply. "It was all my own fault. The place was very like a hill-fort in India. I had got into a good many of these, and I thought I could get into this. The French, however, had a devilish clever fellow there, one Le Breton, and he fairly kept me out. He met me at every point with great spirit and resource. He knocked about the few guns I had, and at last I took to mining—not a bad way either; but, before I could manage it, the enemy collected in force, and I was obliged to retire. "It is odd enough," he added, "that the same men who had defended the place so well, evacuated it in such a hurry the following year when I advanced on Vittoria, that in destroying the defences they blew up a whole battalion of their own people."—*Lord Ellesmere.*

DINNER AT WATERLOO.

It is stated that the Duke of Wellington's cook, named Thornton, was employed all day in the little inn at Waterloo, in preparing the Duke's dinner, and was frequently advised, and even importuned by the wounded and the runaways, to make his escape with the plate and *batterie de cuisine*, but worthy in his way of such a

master, he answered quietly, "I have had the honour
of serving his Grace these six years, and I never yet
knew him to miss a dinner he had ordered, and I don't
think he will to-day." When the Duke returned to eat
the dinner which his confiding cook had prepared for
him, the first person he saw in the room was the illustrious Cambronne (the reputed author of the phrase
La garde meurt et ne se rend pas). This good fellow had
very quietly surrendered himself to a *drummer*, and had
the modesty to think that he might invite himself to the
Conqueror's table. The Duke, however, declined that
honour (with others not less courteously suggested) on
the plea of not knowing how far it might be agreeable
to his Sovereign's ally, the King of France.—*Quarterly
Review*, vol. xc.

THE BEATEN GENERALS.

Before Wellington had an opportunity of measuring
himself with Buonaparte in person, he had beaten in
succession *all* his most eminent Marshals and Lieute-
nants :—*Junot* at Rolica and Vimiero; *Victor*, at Talavera; *Masséna*, at Busaco and Fuentes d'Onor; *Ney*,
during the whole pursuit after Torres Vedras and at
Quatre Bras; *Marmont*, at Salamanca; *Jourdain*, at
Vittoria; *Soult*, everywhere—through Portugal, Spain,
France, Flanders—from Oporto to Waterloo.—*Quarterly
Review*, vol. xc.

CAPTURED GUNS.

I asked the Duke if he could form any calculation of
the number of guns he had taken in the course of his
career. "No," he replied, "not with any accuracy,
somewhere about 3,000, I should guess. At Oporto,
after the passage of the Douro, I took the entire siege

train of the enemy; at Vittoria and Waterloo I took every gun which they had in the field. What however is more extraordinary, *I don't think I ever lost a gun in the field.* After the battle of Salamanca," he went on to explain, " three of my guns attached to some Portuguese cavalry were captured in a trifling affair near Madrid, but they were recovered the next day. In the Pyrenees Lord Hill found himself obliged to throw eight or nine guns over a precipice ; but these also were recovered, and never fell into the enemy's hands at all."—*Lord Ellesmere.*

The Greatest Soldier in the World.

I once asked the Duke (Wellington) whom he considered on the whole the greatest soldier on record. I believe others have asked the same question of him and received the same reply—" Hannibal."—*Lord Ellesmere.*

Wellington as a Statesman.

The appearance of the soldier-senator in Parliament has been thus described by an eye-witness:—"The Duke of Wellington—the Nestor of the Peerage—receives more homage on his way to the House, and has more sway in it, than any other man of the age. Seated at the corner of the leading ministerial bench, on the right of the Chancellor, he is generally engaged reading letters or other documents, many of which he frequently tears to pieces, and strews the fragments round him. At other times he sits with his arms folded and his hat drawn low over his forehead ; he seems to take little heed of the debates, and rarely takes notes; but he is always on the alert, and whenever he rises he breaks the respectful silence which immediately ensues, only to state more briefly, more tersely, and more forcibly than any preceding member, the points which he wishes to urge.   He mostly holds his hat in his hands, and allows it but little quiet.

"His voice betrays that he is in the sear and yellow leaf; and whilst his mind seems as active as ever, it is too evident that the sword outwears the scabbard."

THE WORD OF COMMAND.

I sometimes fear the Duke of Wellington is too much disposed to imagine that he can govern a great nation by word of command in the same way in which he governed a highly disciplined army.   He seems to be unaccustomed to, and to despise the inconsistencies, the weaknesses, the bursts of heroism, followed by prostration and cowardice, which invariably characterise all popular efforts.   He forgets that after all it is from such efforts that all the great and noble institutions of the world have come ; and that on the other hand, the discipline and organization of armies have been only like the flight of the cannon-ball, the object of which is destruction.—*Coleridge's Table Talk.*

NOT TOO MUCH SMOKE.

The Duke of Wellington bought one of Sir William Allan's pictures of the Battle of Waterloo, remarking that it was " Good, very good! not too much smoke!" The artist was requested to call at the Horse Guards on a day appointed to receive payment.   Sir William met his Grace punctually and suggested that to save his invaluable time he should give him a cheque on his bankers for the amount instead of counting out notes and gold.   The first suggestion passed unheeded, and the artist, thinking he had not been heard, repeated it.

The Duke turned round rather sharply and said, "Do you suppose I would allow Coutts's people to know what a fool I had been?"

The Duke's Coat.

In 1845 the Duke called at Nicoll's for a paletôt, which was then something new. The instant he arrived he said, "I have seen the Prince [Prince Albert] wear one of your new kind of coats." The chief puzzle was how to get pockets enough for the great man. Two of them were like the hare pockets of a shooting coat. His request was that the said pockets might be *long and strong*. When he was told that so many pockets destroyed the lightness of the coat, he said, "*It is my wish —it is my wish.*"

Habits of Life.

Wellington was an early riser, simple in his habits, temperate in his diet, and abstemious to the greatest degree; for although he lived at a period when drinking was one of the grossest vices of the day, he was never once known to be guilty of any excess. He was strictly attentive to his person; neat in his dress, but never appeared in gaudy apparel. Had he worn a tenth part of those well-earned honours, which his valorous deeds had gained for him, his breast would have sparkled with brilliants. The badge of the patron Saint of England, the ribbon of the Golden Fleece of Spain, and the unpretending silver medal, bearing the inscription of Waterloo, were the only decorations he was usually in the habit of wearing.—*Three years with the Duke, or Wellington in Private Life.*

o

CHARACTERISTICS.

Important characteristic points in the character of the Duke of Wellington :—

1st. His confidence in himself, and buoyancy under personal responsibility.

2nd. His forbearance and forgiveness of injustice.

3rd. His firmness under home and foreign annoyances.

4th. His natural feelings of secrecy and caution.

5th. His disinterestedness as to money or rank, and his general candour and simplicity of character.

6th. His placability as to the faults and failings of others, evinced by his feelings connected with subordination and courts-martial.—*Introduction to Characteristics of the Duke of Wellington. By Earl de Grey* (1853).

TITLES AND HONOURS.

The Duke of Wellington's titles and honours at his death are thus paraded by the Herald's College:—Arthur Wellesley, the Most High, Mighty, and Most Noble Prince, Duke of Wellington, Marquis of Wellington, Marquis of Douro, Earl of Wellington in Somerset, Viscount Wellington of Talavera, Baron Douro of Wellesley, Prince of Waterloo in the Netherlands, Duke of Ciudad Rodrigo in Spain, Duke of Brunoy in France, Duke of Vittoria, Marquis of Torres Vedras, Count of Vimiero in Portugal, a Grandee of the First Class in Spain, a Privy Councillor, Commander-in-Chief of the British Army, Colonel of the Grenadier Guards, Colonel of the Rifle Brigade, a Field-Marshal of Great Britain, a Marshal of Russia, a Marshal of Austria, a Marshal of France, a Marshal of Prussia, a Marshal of Spain, a Marshal of Portugal, a Marshal of the Netherlands, a

Knight of the **Garter, a** Knight of the Holy Ghost, a Knight of the **Golden** Fleece, a **Knight Grand** Cross of the Bath, a **Knight** Grand Cross of **Hanover, a** Knight of the **Black Eagle,** a Knight of the **Tower and** Sword, a Knight of **St.** Fernando, a **Knight of William of** the **Low Countries,** a Knight of **Charles III., a Knight of** the Sword of Sweden, a **Knight of St. Andrew of Russia,** a Knight of the **Annunciado of Sardinia, a Knight of the** Elephant of **Denmark, a Knight of Maria Theresa, a** Knight of **St. George of** Russia, a **Knight of the** Crown of Rue of **Saxony, a** Knight of **Fidelity of** Baden, a Knight of **Maximilian** Joseph of **Bavaria, a** Knight of St. Alexander **Newsky** of Russia, **a** Knight of **St.** Hermenegilda of Spain, a **Knight of** the Red Eagle of Brandenburgh, a **Knight of** St. Januarius, a **Knight** of the **Golden** Lion of Hesse-Cassel, a Knight of the Lion of **Baden, a Knight of** Merit of Wurtemburgh. The Lord **High Constable of** England, the Constable of the Tower, **the** Constable of Dover Castle, Warden of the **Cinque Ports,** Chancellor of the Cinque **Ports,** Admiral of the **Cinque** Ports, **Lord-Lieutenant** of Hampshire, **Lord-Lieutenant of the** Tower Hamlets, Ranger of St. James's **Park, Ranger of Hyde Park, Chancellor** of the University of **Oxford, Commissioner of the** Royal Military College, Vice-President of the Scottish Naval and Military **Academy, the Master of the Trinity** House, a Governor of **King's College, Doctor of Laws, &c.**

Maxims and Sentences.

The Lord's **Prayer** contains the sum total of religion and **morals.**

Napoleon was indeed a **very** great man, but he was also a very great **actor.**

I do not know which was the best of the French

marshals; but I know that I always found Massena where I least desired that he should be.

Sir John Moore was no pupil of mine; he was as brave as his sword, but he did not know what men could do and could not do.

There are variously shaped heads; now mind mine. It is a square head. I know it, for Chantrey told me so.

Possible! is anything impossible? Read the newspapers.

The army at Waterloo was the worst army ever brought together; my staff was composed of a body of young gentlemen to whom I could entrust no details.

There are no manifestoes like cannon and musketry.

F. M. The Duke of Wellington (this was written in answer to some political busybody) is one of the few persons in this country who don't meddle with things with which they have no concern.

The Duke of Wellington can give no opinion upon that of which he knows nothing.

"What," said a quid nunc, looking up with importance and chattering about Sir De Lacy Evans in Spain, "what will all this produce?" The Duke: "Probably two volumes octavo."

A rough workman came up to the Duke and asked leave to shake hands with him. "Certainly" said the Duke, "I am always happy to shake hands with an honest man."

Surprise may overtake us all. "Were you not," asked a rude questioner, "was not your Grace surprised at Waterloo?" "*No; but I am now!*"

A great country ought never to make little wars.

When war is concluded all animosity should be forgotten.

I would sacrifice Gwalior, or indeed all India, ten

times over, in order to preserve our credit for scrupulous good faith.

I MISTRUST the judgment of every man in a case in which his own wishes are concerned.

BE discreet in all things, and so render it unnecessary to be mysterious about any.

THE history of a battle is like the history of a ball.

HE is most to blame who breaks the law ; no matter what the provocation may be under which he acts.

ONE country has no right to interfere in the internal affairs of another. Non-intervention is the law, intervention is only the exception.

I AM not base enough to allow pillage (to Don Freyre). If you wish your men to plunder, you must name some other General to command them.

IT would undoubtedly be better, if officers placed in the situation in which you were, could correct neglects and errors likely to be attended by consequences fatal to public interests, in language which should not *hurt the feelings* of the person to whom it is addressed; and with a manner divested of vehemence.

WHATEVER may be a man's rank or situation, he ought to be treated with mildness and civility. "Expressions of this sort, harsh language to inferiors," he said, "are not necessary, and they may wound, but they never convince."

I HOLD a high office under Government, but I am not a party man.

WE ought to do great things at this moment, if there was *less of party* and *more of public spirit* in England.

So long as the enemy is in the country we must do all we can to drive him out, whatever may be the constitutional privileges which may be invaded by these measures.

My consolation for the sacrifices which I am called upon to make, I must find in that hope of honourable fame which is to be acquired only by those who, according to the best of their judgment, fallible at the best, pursue the course which leads to the public good.

In regard to the charge of kindness to the enemy, I am afraid it is but too well founded, and that until it is positively ordered by authority, that all enemy's troops in a place taken by storm should be put to death, it will be difficult to prevail upon British officers and soldiers to treat an enemy when they are prisoners otherwise than well.

Better lose ten provinces than sacrifice our reputation for scrupulous good faith, and the good name which we have acquired in the war with the Mahrattas."

Strict justice ought to mark every proceeding of the English East India Company towards the natives.

It is difficult to say what will be successful, and what otherwise, in these governments of intrigue; but, in my opinion, *the broad direct line* is the best.

We ought not to interfere with matters that don't concern us.

It is a sort of privilege of modern Englishmen to read in the daily newspapers lies respecting those who serve them; and I have been so long accustomed to be so treated that I should not have thought it necessary to trouble you on the subject, &c.　．　．　．　I am really quite indifferent respecting what is read of me in the newspapers.

I request you to understand that neither I nor any other officer in the English army, has any right to arrest and to punish magistrates or other persons invested with civil authority.

It is no impulse of vanity which leads me to speak

so highly of my opponent, for it was not I who beat him, but the determined bravery of the English troops, and their unconquerable steadiness.

EVERYTHING of this sort, he wrote, of despatches after victory, ought to be treated in a simple style, without inflation, and, above all, briefly. Such expressions as *Corez sobre os nonuos inimicos* (to succumb to our enemies), don't touch the actual evil. Everybody in Portugal is sufficiently impressed with the danger, and eager to avoid it. We have enthusiasm in plenty, and plenty of cries of *Viva.* We have illuminations, patriotic songs, and *fêtes* everywhere ; but what we want is, that each in his own station, *should do his duty* faithfully, and pay implicit obedience to legal authority.

WHATEVER you think fit to publish, confine yourself to a plain statement of facts and dates, and to such arguments as may be intelligible to every reader.

THE French army is without doubt a wonderful machine.

FRANCE is not an enemy whom I despise, nor does it deserve I should.

I WHO commanded the largest British army employed against an enemy for many years, who had upon my hands the most extensive and difficult concern ever imposed upon any British officer, have not the power of making even a corporal.

I COMMAND the army (1809), yet I have no power to reward, or even to promise a reward.

THAT dish is no doubt excellent, but to tell the plain truth I never care much what I eat. [1]

DON'T be embarrassed (To Richard Oastler, gently

[1] To Cambacères, a renowned gourmet, who immediately cried out, "Good Heavens ! Then what *did* you come here for then ?"

placing his hand on his shoulder). Forget that you are here; we shall never get on if you are embarrassed; fancy that you are talking with one of your neighbours at Fixby, and go on.

WHEN one begins to turn in bed, it is time to get up.

No recriminations nor quarrels in the House or the press will do us (the English) good. I am of the opinion with Napoleon that we had better wash our foul linen at home.

LORD CARDIGAN and Lord Lucan again! (dashing down a mass of correspondence.) By —— these two lords would require a commander-in-chief to themselves. There is no end to their complaints and remonstrances.

ENGLISH soldiers of the steady old stamp, depend upon it there is nothing like them in the world in the shape of infantry.

SOLDIERS not riflemen. We must not allow them to fancy they are *all* riflemen, or they will become conceited, and be wanting to be dressed in green or in some *jack-a-dandy* uniform. Keep to our national uniform and to our solid steady infantry.

DEPEND upon it, gentlemen, the greatest enemies the army has in this country are those who would add unnecessarily to its expense.

THERE is little or nothing in this life worth living for, but we can all of us go straightforward and do our duty.

INDEX.

BBÉ du Pradt, 163.
Absent in Parliament, 99.
Abuse, astonishment at, 25.
Accounts not to be relied on, 111; of Waterloo impossible, 115.
Acquiescence, 14.
Acquitted honourably, 65.
After the battle, 178.
Agitation in Ireland, 142.
Albuera, battle of, 48.
Allies, bad conduct of, 108.
Amildars and officers, 3.
Anecdotes, miscellaneous, 174.
Animosity, 196.
Anonymous letters, 39, 43, 125.
Application, surprising, 98.
Approbation, 14.
Army, British, 25; character of, 136; dissatisfaction in, 25; little discipline in, 71; head of, 89; French, 199.
Arrest of magistrates, 198.
Arthur's, Sir, consideration, 2; and government, 7.
Articles. *Moniteur*, 104.
Assemblies, popular, 30.

Attacking, before, 6.
Attitude of England, 171.
Austrian marriage, 34.
Authorities, independent, 62.

Baba Phurkia, 19.
Back door, 34.
Badajoz, letter from, 32.
Bad egg, 177.
Bad conduct of allies, 108.
Ball and a battle, 110.
Ballot, the, 159.
Battle and a ball, 110; of Waterloo, 109; after, 178: history of, 197; of Toulouse, 91.
Beer bill, 139.
Before attacking, 6.
Begging favours, 128.
Bivouacking, 164.
Bludgeon work, 73.
Bobus Smith, 174.
Boulogne, invasion, 170.
Bourbon party, 87; and peace, 103.
Bribery, 10.
British cavalry, 134.
  ,,   invincibility, 50.
  ,,   moderation, 19.
Brunow, Count, 168.
Buckingham Palace, 138.

Buonaparte, detestation of, 84; tyranny, 47; and French, 81; overturned, 92; and Europe, 97; brought back, 98; hors de la loi, 100; foundation of power of, 103; operations of, 107; fate, 107; death-blow, 106; selfishness of, 163.

CABINET minister, 123.
Calumnies, showers of, 79.
Campaign, review of, 57.
Campbell, Colin, 37; Sir John, 149.
Cardigan, Lord, 200.
Carlos, Don, 164.
Catholics, Irish Roman, 128.
Causes, tracing of, 23.
Cavalry galloping, 51.
Cessation of hostilities, 17.
Champagné, Colonel, 9.
Characteristics of Duke, 194.
Character of Mahrattas, 17.
Charity, 172; reasonable, 21.
Church in Ireland, 130, 142.
Civility, 197.
Claims, service, 13.
Close, Lieut.-Colonel, 4.
Clothing, military, 46.
Coat, Wellington's, 193.
Cock-tailed horse, 46.
Colin Campbell, 37.
Commissariat, 52.
Commissions, Post-office, 152.
Common Council and Wellington, 32.
Complaints, soldiers', 56.
Confinement, solitary, 133.
Consideration for soldiers, 3.
Contagion, 84.
Conversion, death-bed, 172.
Cool Judgment, 41.
Correspondence, 6; of officers, 40.

Country divided, 114.
Court martial, 111.
Cramped by instructions, 93.
Credit, public, 51.

DARLING, Major-Gen., 99.
Dearly-bought glory, 106.
Death-bed conversion, 172.
Debt, imprisonment for, 158.
Dedication, scruples about, 32.
Defence of self, 8.
Defensive, on the, 101.
Delivery of orders, 43.
Desertion, 34.
Difficulties, 172; Spanish, 29.
Difficulty of position, 42.
Disapprobation undeserved, 9.
Discipline of cavalry, 18; foundation of, 51; of army, 59; officers, 60; little real, 71.
Discretion, 197.
Discussions, official, 35; Irish, 124.
Disposition to mercy, 19.
Dissatisfaction in army, 25.
Dissenters, Irish, 130.
Don Carlos, 164.
Drury-lane Theatre, at, 119.
Duende newspaper, 79.
Duke's health, 124; the, at church, 167; praying, 167; smiling in death, 168; sits for portrait, 165, 168; with children, 165; his coolness, 177; Waterloo, after, 178; good night, 169; head, 165; Haydon's letter to, 162; powerless, 199; no party man, 197; characteristics, honours, 194; habits, 193; maxims, 195; and Sir Wm. Allan, 193; and Haydon, 165 *et seq.*; and workmen, 196.

Dungannon, Lady, 175.
Du Pradt, Abbé, 163.
Du Stael, Madme, 163.
Duty, unhesitating, 23; public man's, 20; without mortification, 68.
Duty, 68; of godfather, 117.
Dying of love, 42.
Dynasties, the two, 85.

Economy, real, 14.
Eben, Baron, 39.
England, attitude of, 171; and France, 172; hatred of, 172.
English name disgraced, 13; bravery, 199; quarrels, 200; soldiers, 200.
Enthusiasm, French, 28.
Estate in England, 56.
Esteem, gratifying, 20.
Etiquette, military, 31.
Eton, Wesley at, 174.
Evils of War, 86.
Existing government, 23.

Failure of potatoes, 134.
Faith, good, 198.
False reports, 89.
Famine, Irish, 135.
Favours, begging, 128; received, 44.
Fools and knaves, 7.
Fortified places, 95.
Fortunate man, 65.
Fort William, Bengal, 133.
France, 199; position of, 111; and England, 172; peace with, 170; hates England, 172.
Free press in Malta, 160.
Free trade, 140.
French government, 66; and Buonaparte, 81; neutrality, 96; army, 199.

Gallantry of troops, 50.
Galloping cavalry, 51.
Game laws, 139.
Gentleman, like a, 33.
German troops, 81.
Glory dearly bought, 106.
Godfather, duties of, 117.
Good faith, 198; British, 21.
Goodnight, duke's, 169.
Government and Sir Arthur, 7; the existing, 23.
Governors general, 145.
Gratifying esteem, 20.

Hard pounding, 178.
Hatred of England, 172.
Health, public, 84.
Help unnecessary, 118.
History of a battle, 197.
Honor and interest, 33.
Honourably acquitted, 65.
Honours, 55.
Hospital, orders for, 11.
Hostilities, cessation of, 17.

Impossibilities, military, 83.
Imprisonment for debt, 158.
Inadmissible doctrine, 67.
Indifference, philosophical, 6.
Indolence, Portuguese, 39.
Influence, 197; of woman, 67.
Insurgents, 118.
Interest, promotion by, 76.
Ireland, Roman Catholics in, 128; evil in, 128; invasion of, 126; Church in, 130; Juries' Bill, 143—advantages of, 144; state of, 149; Church Temporalities' Bill, 145; agitation in, 146, 158.
Irish famine, 134; poverty, 132; Protestant petition, 153.
Isolation, 172.

JEWS, emancipation of, 146; not Christians, 147.
Judgment, cool, 41.
Joseph King, 88.
Justice, 112.

KIND letter, 57.
King Joseph, 88.
King, situation of the, 122.
Kings of Spain, 118.
Kittoor, Rajah of, 10.
Knaves and fools, 7.

LAKES, American, 85.
Language of officers, 73.
Laws, Game, 139.
Letter, kind, 51; anonymous, 39, 43.
Libellous nonsense, 40.
Lieut. Wesley, 175.
Life, worth of, 200.
Liverpool, Lord, letter to, 42.
Long marches, 19.
Louis Philippe, 171.
Love, dying of, 42.
Lowe, Sir Hudson, 121.
Loyal support, 151.
Lucan, Lord, 200.
Lusitanian legion, 44.

MAGISTRATES, arrest of, 198.
Magnates, Indian, 12.
Mahratta country, 1; truth, 19.
Mahratta's character, 17.
Majesty, 64.
Malcolm, to Major, 17; colonel, 32.
Malta, 161.
Manifestoes, 196.
Man, "rights of men," 6; fortunate, 65.
Marches, long, 19.

Marriage, Austrian, 34.
Match, pounding, 108.
Maxims, 195.
Medal question, 80.
Mercy, disposition, 18.
Metamorphosis of Nelson, 151.
Military, civil editing of, 49; impossibilities, 83.
Militia, 151.
Minister, Cabinet, 123.
Miscellaneous Anecdotes, 174.
Mischief of Irish discussions, 124.
Mis-statement, 124.
Mistakes, Waterloo, 116.
Mob, remedy for, 117.
Moderation, British, 19.
Modesty, 23.
Money, prize, 16.
Moore, Sir John, 196.
Mortars (in siege), 75.
Movements of large bodies, 16.
Munro, letter to, 1, 16.

NAPOLEON, 195; Louis, 170; Buonaparte, 163.
National passion, 141.
Natives, conduct of, 1; ideas of time, 4; trading with, 4; marriages, 15.
Necessity for secresy, 37.
Nelson, Lord, 150.
Neutrality, French, 96.
Newspaper paragraphs, 28.
Newspapers and slave trade, 97; harm, 78; libel, 79; lies, 113, 198; Moniteur, 104.
Nonsense, libellous, 40.

O'CONNELL, Mr., 126; prosecution of, 127.
Officers, inexperience of, 60; change of, 61; removal of,

63; language of, 73; require to be kept in order, 45; intriguing, 123.

Operations, continuing, **107.**

Orange, Prince of, 69.

Orders, British, 68; delivery of, 43; for hospital, 11.

PAINE's Rights of Man, 136.

Palace, Buckingham, 138.

Paragraphs, newspaper, 38.

Paris, things in, 114.

Party, Bourbon, **87;** spirit, 15; men, **197.**

Passion, national, **141.**

Peace and the Bourbons, 103.

  „ the object of government, 91.

Peroune, 108.

Peshwar, 11, 12.

Philippe, Louis, 171.

Philosophical indifference, 6.

Philosophy, 9.

Pillage, 197.

Placability, 194.

Places, fortified, 95.

Plunder, 164; and rapine, 35.

Police Bill, 138.

Politics, study of, **172.**

Popular assemblies, **30.**

Portuguese, 39; character of, **43.**

Position of army at Waterloo, 104; of France, **111.**

Post Office Bill, 152.

Potato crop, failure of, 134.

Pounding match, 108.

Poverty, Irish, **139.**

Powers of Europe, **109.**

Prayer, Lord's, 195.

Predatory war, 14.

Press, the, 170; free in Malta, 160.

Prince Talleyrand, 140.

Prize money, 16.

Proclamation to Spaniards, 54.

Procuring intelligence, 104.

Promotion by interest, 76; claims for, 35.

Property, security of, 164.

Protestant population, 129; sovereigns in Europe, 132; petition, Irish, 153.

Provost duty, 25.

Public credit, 51; health, 84; affairs, secrecy, 12; spirit, 197.

Public traducers, 70.

Punishment, 37.

QUEEN VICTORIA's household, 155; consort, 156; speech, 157.

Question, both sides of, 24; medal, 80; slavery, **95.**

RAILWAYS, 151.

Rancourt, Mdlle., **97.**

Rapine and plunder, **35.**

Real economy, **14.**

Recollections, **112.**

Recruiting, best way of, 77.

Recruits, 63; German, 81.

Redactor newspaper, 80.

Remains of French army, 106.

Remedy for mob, **127.**

Removal of officers, 62.

Reports, false, 89.

Responsibility, 14.

Review of campaign (1812), 57.

"Rights of Men" man, 6.

Risk in actions, 10.

Roman Catholics in Ireland, 128; disabilities, 137.

Rosy and dosy, 166.

Rules, submission to, 17.

Russia, Emperor of, **122.**

Salamanca, 52.
Sale of beer, 138.
Scenes, death-bed, 172.
Sebastian, plunder of, 78.
Second in command, 62.
Secrecy, necessity for, 37.
Sentiments, favour of Spanish, 24.
Service claims, 13; public, 4.
Shawe, 17.
Shower of calumnies, 79.
Shrapnel's shells, 49.
Siege, military, 75.
Slavery, 144; question, 95; abolition of bill, 148.
Slave trade, 94; abolition of, 97; traffic, 134; West India, 144.
Slovenly business, 65.
Smith, Bobus, 174.
Soldiers' solitary confinement, 133; complaints, 56; old, 63; English, 200; weight of, 176.
Soult, Marshal, 88.
Southey, Mr., 121; and Peninsular war, 120.
Spain, kings of, 118; disease of, 38; withdrawal from, 54; services to, 67.
Spaniards, proclamation to, 51.
Spanish slavery, 75; character, 72; conduct, 41; energy, 53; and France, 33; revolution, 57.
Spirit, party, 15; want of, 35.
Stein, M. de, 102.
Stuart, Charles, 38.
Style, simple, 199.
Success, military, 74.
Supposing, 176.
Surprise, 196.

Talleyrand, Prince, 140.
Temporalities' Bill, 145.

Test Act 136.
Theocracy in Ireland, 129.
Time, 17; military, 5; native ideas of, 4.
Torrens, Lieut.-Col., 36.
Toulouse, battle of, 91,
Trades' unions, 159.
Traducers, public, 70.
Traffic, slave, 134.
Tranquillity, 38.
Troops, raw, 14; gallantry of, 50; German, 82.
Truth, Marhatta, 19.
Tyranny, Buonaparte's, 47.

Unhesitating duty, 23.
Unions, trades', 159.
Unnecessary help, 118.

Value, full to be given, 102.
Victoria's, Queen, household, 155.
Villiers, Hon. J., 33.
Vimiero, action, 24.
Vittoria, 70; medals, 90.
Volumes in 8vo., 196.

Want, national, 72; of spirit, 35.
War, predatory, 14; conclusion of, 20, 35; evils of, 86; a little, 159; risk of, 171.
Water and pepper, 18.
Waterloo, battle of, 109; position of army at, 104; mistakes of, 116; again, 115; true account of, impossible, 115; mistakes concerning, 118; after, 178; army at, 196.
Weight of soldiers, 176.
Wellington, characteristics, 194; habits, 193; honours, 194; maxims of, 195: coat of, 193; and Haydon, 165;

Wm. Allan, Sir, 193; at church, 167; at prayers, 167; head of, 165; Waterloo, after, 178; and workmen, 196; hook nose of, 177; hard pounding, 178; Sir John Moore, 196.

Wesley, Lieut., 175.
Westmeath magistrates, 141.
William IV., 153.
Withdrawal from Spain, 54.
Women, influence of, 67.
Wonderful times, 172.
Worship, soldiers', 29.

CHISWICK PRESS :—PRINTED BY WHITTINGHAM AND WILKINS,
TOOKS COURT, CHANCERY LANE.